THE
BOY
AT THE
KEYHOLE

Center Point
Large Print

Books are produced in the United States using U.S.-based materials

Books are printed using a revolutionary new process called THINKtech™ that lowers energy usage by 70% and increases overall quality

Books are durable and flexible because of Smyth-sewing

Paper is sourced using environmentally responsible foresting methods and the paper is acid-free

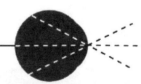

This Large Print Book carries the Seal of Approval of N.A.V.H.

THE
BOY
AT THE
KEYHOLE

STEPHEN GILES

CENTER POINT LARGE PRINT
THORNDIKE, MAINE

This Center Point Large Print edition
is published in the year 2018 by arrangement with
Harlequin Books S.A.

The text of this Large Print edition is unabridged.
In other aspects, this book may vary
from the original edition.
Printed in the United States of America
on permanent paper.
Set in 16-point Times New Roman type.

ISBN: 978-1-64358-017-3

Library of Congress Cataloging-in-Publication Data

The Library of Congress has cataloged record
under LCCN 2018042463

THE
BOY
AT THE
KEYHOLE

For Mary Giles,
my mother

1

The morning light was disappointing, spilling faintly across the stone floor and making very little of the shattered bowl or its contents. It was hard to know for certain, not without checking, but there were probably clouds overhead, because now and then a great beam of sunlight would push through the mullioned windows, spotlighting the kitchen table and the boy sitting on it. Samuel looked into these brief flares of honeycombed light with a kind of spellbound curiosity—the dust particles churned around the bleeding wound on his leg like a swarm of bees. It was confusing more than anything. She hated dust; everybody knew that. Yet Samuel was forced to consider the possibility that Ruth's kitchen wasn't really as spotless as she claimed.

"Didn't I ask you to stop running about?"

Samuel nodded. Ruth had asked that question three times already and each time he had answered it the same way. She was like that sometimes, asking the same thing over and again. Did she really suppose his answer might change from one moment to the next? That he'd suddenly say that she hadn't asked him to stop running about? He wasn't stupid.

"Kitchens aren't for playing in." Ruth was

crouching on the floor picking up the pieces of ceramic bowl. She placed them on the table beside Samuel, where they rocked gently back and forth. "This was my best bowl, Samuel, and it's not as if I can go into the village and buy another." She looked up at him. "Who do you suppose I was making the cake for?" Before Samuel could answer, Ruth said, "Not me, that's for certain."

The boy was silent.

"I should think this house has enough rooms to make a racket in without bringing it in here. Truly, Samuel, you make so much noise I sometimes wonder if you're possessed."

"What's *possessed* mean?" said Samuel.

"It means a boy who doesn't have the good sense to stop."

Once she was done picking up the shattered bowl, Ruth grabbed a bucket and a rag and got to work on the chocolate cake mix that had settled on the floor like a lava flow.

Samuel's attention returned to the cut on his shin. A small amount of blood oozed from the wound and the boy scooped it up with his finger. Samuel never failed to be disappointed by the touch of blood—it held so much promise when it was seeping from a wound, red and thick and ghoulish, but then you touched it and it seemed to fade to nothing, leaving barely a stain on your fingertips.

"It looks worse than it is." That was another

thing Ruth had repeated several times that morning. "It's not at all deep. Heal in no time." She sniffed. "Does it hurt?"

Samuel shook his head. It did hurt but he knew not to say so.

"Good," Ruth said. "I'll clean it up and then you can get out from under my feet."

She went into the larder and came out with a small bottle and a fresh cotton swab. By then the restless clouds had shifted again, bleeding the light from the room and throwing smoky shadows across Ruth's face. Samuel once heard his mother describe Ruth as a "handsome woman," but to him she just looked bothered.

"You must try to be good, Samuel." Ruth unscrewed the glass bottle and poured a small amount onto the swab. "Running this house by myself and looking after you is hard enough without . . ." She dabbed the wound on Samuel's leg and the boy did his best not to wince. "I just wanted you to sit down and eat your breakfast. Didn't I ask you to stop running about? Didn't I warn you that I was in no mood for nonsense?"

Samuel nodded.

"Well," said Ruth, wiping the last traces of blood away, "what's done is done. Let's say no more about it." Her voice was always softest then, her head bent low to meet Samuel's, her eyes seeking his out. She pushed the hair from his brow. "Friends?"

Samuel nodded. "When is Mother coming home?"

Ruth sighed. "Please don't start that, Samuel. Not today."

"Why hasn't she—?"

The back door opened and Olive stepped in, taking off her coat and apologizing to Ruth for being late. "The bus didn't turn up and I had to walk up from the village."

"I see." Ruth slipped the bottle of antiseptic into her pocket and patted her brown hair. "I tried to call you this morning, Olive, but the phone just rang out."

Olive came in every Saturday to help with the cleaning. Back before Samuel had started school, the house had two maids, a cook and a full-time gardener. Now it was just Ruth with Olive once a week and William doing what he could with the garden on Wednesdays and Thursdays.

"I walked Ma to the market," said Olive, hanging up her coat. "We were meant to go yesterday but Ma was feeling ill so—" Olive stopped suddenly. "What happened to your leg, Master Samuel?"

Olive wasn't supposed to call the boy that. His mother didn't allow fancy titles. She was American and had all sorts of ideas about that sort of thing. Samuel knew the story by heart—from the moment his mother had married his father and moved from New York, she was determined that *her* English home would not suffer under the soul-crushing burden of formality. Samuel had no idea what that meant but he was certain it had something to do with his mother being daring.

"I hit the table," said Samuel.

"How did you manage that?" said Olive.

The hair fell across Samuel's eyes. "I fell."

"He was running around with one of his planes and tripped over the chair," said Ruth, helping Samuel off the table. "It's not a bad cut—he'll be good as new in no time."

"I'm glad to hear it." Olive said this without taking her eyes off Samuel. "You're okay, then?"

"Why shouldn't he be? It's just a cut." Ruth cleared her throat. "Olive, as I was trying to say—the reason I telephoned this morning was to tell you that I won't be needing you today. I'm very sorry you've had to come all of this way."

"Oh?" said Olive.

"The thing is, I doubt very much I'll need your services again," said Ruth.

Samuel watched the way Olive's eyes darted about, landing on him or the floor or Ruth but never settling for more than a second before flying off to the next thing.

"You don't want me to come anymore?" said Olive.

"If I had my way I would have you here all week," Ruth said. "But as you know, that is impossible at the present time . . . with things as they are."

"I'd be glad to stay on and we can settle up when Mrs. Clay returns?"

"I don't know when that will be, Olive."

"It'll be soon," Samuel said. "It'll be soon, won't it, Ruth?"

"Yes, I hope so." Ruth looked at Olive and the scowl fell from her face. "You're an excellent worker and I will gladly give you a reference. If there was any other way . . ."

Olive lifted her head then and didn't look quite so mousy. "Is William to stay on?"

"Samuel, why don't you go and ride your bike?" Ruth had a way of asking that didn't leave room for any answer but one. "Change your shoes first—the grass is probably still wet from last night."

"I like these shoes." Samuel felt it necessary to fold his arms.

"All the better to keep them from getting damp," said Ruth.

Samuel considered some kind of protest but it wasn't the day for it.

"Hurry along, Samuel," said Ruth, before offering Olive a chair at the table. They sat down, huddled together and immediately started talking in low voices. Samuel guessed it was about money. That's why his walk from the kitchen was a slow one; he practically willed his ears to reach back and scoop up the hushed words passing between those two. Usually talk about money would lead to talk about his mother. And he wanted to hear news of her so badly it sometimes made his whole body ache. But rooms are never as long as you need them to be and Samuel soon reached the door. He crouched down and looked busy with his shoelaces but Ruth was having none of that.

"Off you go. And change those shoes."

Samuel passed through the hall and climbed the staircase like he was heading to the gallows. If they were talking about his mother why shouldn't he hear what they were saying? She belonged to him, didn't she? The whole trouble about money had something to do with her and why she'd been away so long—one hundred and thirteen days to be exact. Hadn't he been wishing and praying for her to come home day and night? And if they were going to sit there and whisper about her, talking among themselves as if she was their concern and not his, then what choice did he have but to try and listen in? He knew that adults had their secrets and there were some things he didn't need to know. Ruth had told him so a hundred times. But rather like the dust he'd discovered in her kitchen, the boy was starting to realize that just because a thing is said, it didn't make it true.

2

Samuel always ran home after school. Mostly Joseph would run with him despite his view that hills were ludicrous things that didn't warrant running up. Joseph was his best friend, though sometimes Samuel worried that such a title was fraudulent due to the fact that Joseph was his only friend. Still, his father used to say you only need one good friend in life. Joseph lived in the gatehouse at Braddon Hall, which was just over the hill from Samuel's place. His mother cooked for the lord's family and his father worked the land there.

"I don't see why we have to run home every day like it's the bloody Olympics." Joseph dropped his school bag on the grass and spat. "Walking will get you there just the same."

Samuel never could explain it. How he ran home every day with a tempest whirling in his chest. And that it was hope. Hope that today his mother would be there waiting for him. Or that another postcard would come from her. That he would hear something, anything, and know where she was now and, most important of all, when she was coming home. But you don't say such things aloud, even to a best friend.

"I like to run," was his reply.

"Well, that's barmy," said Joseph, wiping the sweat from his chin.

Samuel's house crested the hill and there was always a certain amount of pain at the steepest point—more so today because his shin, which Ruth had covered that morning, still ached. But he pushed on, practically leaping through the open gates when he reached the house.

"Meet you here at eight?" called Joseph from behind him.

Samuel nodded. They walked to school together every morning.

He walked quickly up the drive, the crunch of the gravel beneath his feet never failing to satisfy him. His gaze was fixed on the house, and though it was tempting, he didn't steal so much as a sideways glance at the kitchen garden with hopes of spotting his rabbit. He looked only at the house. Though it wasn't the equal of Braddon Hall, the building was still vast and rather formidable. It sat on the outskirts of the village on what had once been a large estate. All of the farmland had been sold after his father died and now the stables stood empty and the only other buildings were the woodshed and the main house with its two square wings of pale yellow stone, its rows of large sash windows in groups of three and its forest of chimney pots sprouting across the roofline.

Samuel dropped his school bag and coat on the

checkered floor, taking off his hat and flinging it on top of the bag, and then raced down the hall. He stopped abruptly. Turned around and hurried back, pushing the door closed—gently. Ruth didn't tolerate open front doors and she didn't tolerate slamming doors, either.

By the time he reached the back of the house, he was moving at what he considered an ideal speed. But there was a left turn into the kitchen and it came sooner than he anticipated. He skidded across the floor, hit the wall with his shoulder and lurched into the room.

Ruth was at the kitchen table kneading a lump of dough. She didn't look up. "I would think you'd know better than to storm into my kitchen like you're running from a burning building."

"Sorry, Ruth," said Samuel. "Did Mother—?"

"Just what are you doing with that tie?" Ruth said. "It's the second one you've needed this year, and there won't be a third, so you'd be wise to take better care of it."

Samuel looked down. His school tie was balled up in his fist. He apologized again and set it down on the bench beside him.

"How was school, then?" asked Ruth.

The boy shrugged. "Okay."

"Such enthusiasm, Samuel." The boy watched as Ruth rolled the dough, pushing it down with her fists, her face locked in a grimace. A strand of her wavy brown hair had come loose and she blew it out of her eyes. "I'm making shortbread for the market, though I'm sure I can spare a few if you're good. After tea, of course. Homework?"

"Some," said Samuel. "Did she come?" It was a stupid question, he knew that. But he couldn't help from asking it. "Is Mother back? Is she upstairs?"

"Do you suppose I'd let you stand here talking about homework and shortbread if Mrs. Clay had come home?" Ruth stole a brief glance at Samuel. "She'll let you know when she's coming home, I'm sure of that."

"Then why hasn't she?" Samuel's eyes narrowed. "How can she stay away so long? It's been over sixteen weeks, that's one hundred and fifteen days."

"I've told you—there's no sense in counting the days, Samuel. It'll only get you worked up and we know how that goes."

Samuel crossed his arms then. "I will count them, every single one."

"Suit yourself. Your mother might be finished with those bankers any day now—but America's an awful long way. It's not like catching a train." She smiled but like always it wasn't entirely convincing. "You should know that better than anyone—you're always poring over that book of maps."

"It's an atlas."

"I stand corrected." Ruth licked her lips. "Look,

I know it doesn't make it any easier but your mother has a lot of very important matters to attend to, and when you're on a big trip like she is, I expect time just runs away on you."

"Doesn't she want to come home?" Samuel's voice was barely a whisper.

Ruth didn't answer right away; she seemed to be thinking. Then she said, "Well, of course she does. What a thing to say."

Samuel felt a great tide of anger rising up toward his mouth. He knew better than to yell but he felt certain there are some things a boy couldn't be expected to control. Because sometimes it seemed as if the more he missed his mother, the more he loved her, the farther away she got. "She didn't even say goodbye," he said, coming as close to shouting as he dared. "Why would she do that, Ruth? She just left while I was sleeping. She didn't say goodbye."

"Samuel Clay, lower your voice." Ruth took her hands off the dough and a cloud of flour rose up toward her face. "You know very well why your mother didn't say goodbye. The trip to America was very sudden and she had to be in London by the morning, which meant leaving here in the dead of night. I helped her pack in a great hurry and I know for a fact she looked in on you, sat on your bed and stroked your face. But she didn't want to wake you because you were sleeping so soundly."

"She hasn't written a letter. Not one."

"What about those postcards you love so much?"

Samuel looked down at his school shoes. "It's not the same thing."

"Does that mean you wouldn't be interested in receiving another one?"

This caused a spark to light up behind Samuel's green eyes. "You mean?"

Ruth nodded, returning to the dough. "I put it on your bed."

Samuel had no time to respond; he was already running for the stairs.

3

Boston Harbor sparkled like gemstones under a sun so perfectly round and golden it looked like an egg yolk. Samuel sat down on the bed, the postcard wrapped between his fingers. He always studied the picture first, leaving his mother's handwritten note until last. It was like enjoying the roast chicken while every part of you could hardly wait for the dessert. His mother's note was always dessert. But like any delicious treat, once it was within reach, it proved impossible to resist.

Samuel turned the card over. His eyes swept across her ornate handwriting and he felt that familiar rush, warm and quick, washing through him. Her hand had pressed each and every letter onto that postcard. She had probably sat at a desk in her hotel room or in a tea shop somewhere, thinking only of him, and writing this message. These were her words. Her words, just for his eyes. Samuel took a breath and started reading as slowly as he could manage.

July 20, 1961
Dearest Samuel,
    How I miss you, my little man. I have arrived in Boston and it is damp and dreary, just like my spirits. As

yet there is no end in sight to my business here in America. But I promise that I will be home as soon as I am able. Be good for Ruth.

With love and kisses,
Mother

The last he heard she was still in New York. Now she had moved on to Boston. He would need to update the atlas. Samuel turned the card over, then over again, as if he might find some other message from his mother, something hidden that might offer a clue. People did that sometimes— plant clues. But there was nothing. *No end in sight to my business here.* Why was there no end in sight? Why was it taking so long?

Samuel knew that there had been a lot of trouble with the steel mill in Lincolnshire. They owed more than owned, that's what his father always said. Then after he died, the banks, which were run by appalling men with ice-cold hearts, expected his mother to sell everything, accept her losses and walk away. But his mother had a head for numbers; that's another thing his father used to say. And so she had gone to every corner of England trying to raise something she called *capital.* When that didn't work, she decided to try her luck in America. Samuel's grand-father lived in New York, though Samuel had never met him, on account of the old man being sour as a lemon. Samuel's father said that, as well.

I will be home as soon as I am able. She promised that at the end of every postcard. There had been eight in all, including this latest one. All declaring that she would come home *as soon as I am able.* What did that mean? Why wasn't she free to come home whenever she chose? Was someone holding her against her will? He hoped not. Well, mostly. A small part of him, a wicked part he was certain, wished that she had been locked away. Perhaps by his grandfather, who hated the English. Or one of those American bankers. Because then it wouldn't be her choice to be away so long.

Samuel put the card down on the bed, then picked it up again. Waiting for someone to come home was an awful thing. The boy sighed. Then he turned it over and began reading again.

" 'Be good for Ruth. With love and kisses, Mother.' " Samuel took a drink of milk and wiped his mouth. "Shall I read it again?"

"You'll wear the ink out if you keep reading it over." Ruth was using an empty peach tin to press the dough into circles, which were the only shape shortbread ought to be, as far as Samuel was concerned. "Still, I'm glad you know where your mother is and that she's well."

"I wonder what Boston is like," said Samuel.

"The head housekeeper at the first home I

worked in, Mrs. Delaney, she'd been the governess for a family from Boston in her younger years. She said they were ghastly."

"Are all the people from Boston ghastly?"

"I doubt it. People are much the same everywhere you go—good and bad and everything in between."

"Do you think Mother will be there long?" Samuel had propped the postcard against a large jar of flour and was gazing into the picture of Boston Harbor.

"How should I know, Samuel? You wanted to hear from your mother and now you have— be glad of that." Ruth tried to sound stern but Samuel thought she sounded rather pleased. "It's a lovely card and mind what she says about being good for me."

"She hates it there and wants to come home, that's what she says." Samuel picked up the card and turned it over. " 'I have arrived in Boston and it is damp and dreary, just—' "

" 'Just like my spirits,' " said Ruth, interrupting him. "I know it by heart myself, you've read it out so many times. Let's talk of something else."

Ruth could do that. Make a decree, like a queen or something, that certain topics had reached their end and that would be that.

"I won't read it aloud again because you don't want me to," Samuel said, "but Mother says she misses me and that she wants to come home. That's what she says."

"Of course she wants to come home." Ruth set aside the peach tin and began to place the cut pieces of dough onto a baking tray. "But as I've told you too many times to count, before she can, your mother has important business to see to."

"Doesn't she know how long it will take?" said Samuel. "She must have some idea when—"

"Why must she? These things are very complicated and . . ." Ruth sighed. "Your mother is seeking a large investment and bankers don't hand over big sums of money without giving it a great deal of thought."

"Why doesn't she ever tell me where she's staying so that I can write back?" A frown had set in, the boy's nostrils flaring. "Why, Ruth?"

"Well, I can't say for certain." Ruth cleared her throat the way she always did when something was making her uncomfortable. "Perhaps she didn't think of it or she isn't properly settled in yet, and if she did tell you, well, I expect she wouldn't have the time to be answering letters."

"I'll telephone her, then," declared Samuel.

Ruth rolled her eyes. "Don't they teach you anything at that village school? I can hardly get a call through to my sister in Surrey without a dozen operators and an earful of crackle, let alone America."

"I'll send her a telegram. You don't need a dozen operators for that, do you?" He nodded. "I'll send a telegram to Boston and ask her when she's coming home."

Ruth smiled faintly. "And how are you planning to do that? As you've just been grumbling, you haven't a clue which hotel she's staying at."

The boy glanced up at the housekeeper and his face was now a mask of suspicion. "Do you know?"

"Me?" Ruth's mouth dropped open and she huffed. "If I knew that, I'd be sending her a telegram myself so that you'd stop asking me these infernal questions."

When Samuel got worked up about his mother, all sorts of thoughts bubbled up in his mind. Sometimes they were just things he felt— the ache of missing her or the resentment that she was gone. Other times they were things he wanted to know. Things he had a right to know. And he would ask them, even when a part of him dreaded what the answers might be.

"Why didn't Mother take me with her? If she knew she was going to be away for so long, why did she leave me here?"

Ruth stopped placing the dough onto the tray. "You think too much, young man. Naturally your mother wanted you with her—there's no question about that—but how could she take all of those important meetings with you by her side?"

"You could have come, too," said Samuel.

"And who would look after this house?"

"Olive," said Samuel.

"Enough." Ruth's voice was low and firm. "I won't have you working yourself into a state. We know how that ended last time."

Samuel remembered. He had gotten upset and said things and done things that had made Ruth cross—and there had been consequences. So, he knew he should stop. Only, he couldn't. "I want to call Uncle Felix."

Ruth stood up. "Whatever for?"

"He might have heard something. He might know where Mother is staying or when she's coming home."

His uncle Felix was his father's only brother, and though Samuel didn't see him a great deal, he liked him well enough. Felix would play cricket with him and sneak him extra sweets and make a joke of almost everything. But since his father died Uncle Felix hadn't been around much. He lived just a few miles away in Penzance, but being pathologically sociable, he was rarely home.

"I spoke to your uncle just last week and he's had no word from your mother." Ruth walked to the oven and slid the tray inside. "In fact, he was envious of your postcards."

"I want to talk to Uncle Felix," said Samuel again.

"You're not going to bother him with this nonsense." Ruth wiped her brow and Samuel saw that the flour had coated her hands like a pair of gloves. "I'm running this house single-handedly and I've got more important things to do than argue with the likes of you, Samuel Clay. Take yourself up to your room and change out of that school uniform and then see to your homework."

Samuel knew the stern look on Ruth's face very well—it meant there was no room for argument and that her patience had reached its end. So he stood up. But he pushed the chair back in such a way that its hard scraping along the stone floor would demonstrate his condemnation, without resorting to backchat. Ruth didn't tolerate backchat.

"Put that chair under the table just like you found it," Ruth said.

The boy did as he was told.

"That's more like it. Now off you go. March."

Samuel walked quickly from the room, his face a storm of grievances, and he knew, even though he didn't have eyes in the back of his head, that Ruth was watching him leave the whole time.

4

He didn't go to his room and change out of his school uniform, not right away. Instead, Samuel took his mother's postcard to the study at the far end of the house. This room was where his father did most of his worrying, and after he died, all of those worries were handed to Samuel's mother, so she took the study for herself. She had removed the heavy curtains and had the dark bookshelves painted white—stocking them with all the books she had brought with her from America. To cheer the place up, she said.

Whenever Samuel entered the room his eyes tended to fall on all the empty spaces. The mahogany cabinet where his father kept his papers, the pair of vases with shells on them and the paintings of Greek myths. They were all gone now, sold and shipped out, because there were bills to pay and what good is a painting or a vase without a house to put them in? There were empty spaces like this all over the house. Samuel wasn't very interested in the old paintings or vases but he did wonder where they were now and if they were happy. Which he knew was stupid.

Next to his mother's desk, by the bay window, was a small table. On it sat a very large book. The atlas had been a gift from Samuel's father to his mother—no one knew why—and even though she never really looked at it much, she kept it there by her desk. Samuel supposed this was on account of it being a treasure.

The atlas was open at a double page. There was England, France, Spain and parts of Africa on one side, the Atlantic Ocean in the middle, and the Americas on the other. The atlas had a crowd of pins stuck in it with tiny green flags at the top—green being his mother's favorite color—marking all the places she had been on her journey through America and Canada: California, Texas, Florida, Pennsylvania, Toronto, New York. Across the sea there was another pin fixed into the page, this one with a white tag. It was planted in West Cornwall, on the outskirts of Penzance, which was as close to their village as Samuel could manage.

Even though the atlas was his mother's, it was Samuel's father who had taught him to use the book. When Samuel was four or five—he wasn't exactly sure—his mother went away to Bath for a rest. She was very tired so she went to a place where there would be peace and quiet and time to breathe. Samuel had once heard his father talking to Uncle Felix on the telephone and he said that Margot—that was Samuel's mother's name—was not suited to domestic life. He said that she had a restless soul. When Samuel asked what that meant, his father had ruffled Samuel's hair and told him it meant his mother was always looking around the next corner, waiting for the next thing. What was the next thing? His father had smiled, though he didn't look especially cheerful, and said he really didn't know.

While she was away Samuel missed her very much. He would look out of the window, waiting for her return all day and call for her in the night, as if his cries would carry her from Bath and spirit her back to him. Asking again and again where she was and when she was coming back and why she was gone. He was always like that with his mother—even when she was near him it was never quite near enough. So his father showed him the atlas, planting a pin in West Cornwall near where their house was and another in Bath, where his mother was resting.

"Now you can see how close she is," his father had said.

And though it was just a drawing on a page and a few pins, seeing where she was and how small the distance was between them made Samuel feel better. Just a little. He did try to understand, about his mother being a restless soul and always looking around the next corner, but sometimes it felt like she was always some-place else. Traveling, resting, visiting friends, taking a break to do something his parents called *rejuvenate*. After his father died, Samuel's mother disappeared again. His father had fallen one night coming home from his club, hitting his head on the front steps of their home in Berkeley Square. Samuel's mother said that her husband didn't drink to excess as a general rule, but he was especially sad because the London house, which had belonged to his grandfather and was therefore horribly sentimental, was to be sold under orders from a group of scoundrels she called the creditors.

She stayed away for seven weeks and three days. In London, mostly, settling things up. She wrote to Samuel two times, short letters commenting on the rain and how there was a great mess that needed sorting out. So Samuel had stuck a pin in London and looked at the atlas every day, reminding himself that his mother was barely a hand's length away, which wasn't so very far when you thought of it like that.

And now she was gone again. She didn't want to go away—she hadn't planned it—but then business was like that, wasn't it? No, she didn't want to go away. But who was going to fix things, if not her?

Samuel opened the drawer of his mother's desk and retrieved the box of pins. His father had cut the colored tags for him, storing them in an empty box of matches, so he selected a green one and attached it to the top of the pin. Then he located Boston on the map and pushed the pin down into the paper like he was planting a flag. His eyes traveled over all the cities she had visited in the exact order she had visited them, landing, finally, in Boston. Where she was at that very moment. He wondered what she was doing right now and if she thought of him as endlessly as he thought of her. He figured she must.

He was here and she was there, and even though it didn't look so very far away, Samuel couldn't pretend she was as close as a hand or even a forearm. After all, he was nine now. Once more, the boy took the voyage across the sea, this time from Boston to Cornwall, his finger drifting back and forth across the Atlantic, marking out the miles as he went and all the distance between them.

5

After Samuel had changed out of his school uniform, his mind turned to places he had no business being. This presented something of a challenge because Ruth had a knack for being everywhere all at once. He would need to be careful. Which is why the door to his bedroom opened with great caution. Samuel stuck his head out, peering up and down. It wasn't quite dinnertime but the sun had dropped away and now the only thing passing through the windows were shadows, fixing themselves along the long corridor like curtains of milky gloom.

Samuel was hoping to hear Ruth in the kitchen clunking pots and pans or opening cupboards. But it was too far away and all he heard was his own breaths and the grandfather clock at the far end of the hallway. He walked carefully, which he knew was stupid, because wasn't he allowed to be walking down the hall? And besides, he hadn't done anything he wasn't supposed to yet. With that in mind, his stride picked up and he walked as carefree as he could manage, even running his hand along the paneled wall as he went, which he felt was something a boy with nothing to hide would do.

He had just passed Ruth's bedroom when he

stopped and backed up. The door was closed, same as always. Samuel pressed his ear to the door and heard nothing of interest. Being a housekeeper, Ruth's bedroom was supposed to be in the servants' quarters at the back of the kitchen. But Samuel's mother thought that was a terrible idea; it would certainly make Ruth feel like a slave or, at very least, a second-class citizen. And how could you expect someone as proud as Ruth to sleep in some little room with hardly a window and still keep her dignity? If she was a part of the family, which she was, then she should be treated as such. Samuel's mother couldn't manage without Ruth. She was her right arm, that's what she said, with a gift for keeping everything at the house humming along so that Samuel's mother was free to worry about far more important things.

Samuel walked on, passing two more doors and then stopping in front of the next. He looked up and down the corridor one more time, which is what you did when you wanted to be certain. Now that he stood on the precipice of this wrongdoing, he felt the fluttering in his chest that made every breath sound as if he were sitting on a rattling train. Samuel bit his bottom lip and told himself that some rules made no sense and why shouldn't he do this, which was hardly a great crime, was it? In fact, it was no crime at all. He reached for the doorknob. The brass handle felt cold against his skin, and though Samuel refused to admit it, this felt like an admonishment. As if the doorknob knew what he was up to and didn't approve. With a twist and the feeblest of squeaks the door opened—what choice did it have?—and the boy stepped inside, closing it carefully behind him.

A mother's bedroom is always pretty, at least in books and things. But not his mother's. She preferred white walls and dark furniture, just a chair by her dressing table, a chest of drawers, plain curtains on the windows. She liked things simple and unadorned and found frills of any kind, and floral frills in particular, utterly demoralizing.

Though she hadn't been in the room for a long time, there were traces of his mother there. The hint of her perfume and cigarettes, the scent of her leather gloves, her creams, which were arranged on the dressing table. Only the softest spray of moonlight wandered about the chamber, so Samuel turned on a lamp by the bed. When it was lit up, the bedroom was simple, unfussy and still. Couldn't he just picture his mother sitting at the dressing table putting on a necklace or applying her face cream or dabbing her neck with perfume and couldn't he hear the melody of her voice as she chatted with his father or Ruth about this or that?

The room had once been both his mother and his father's room and there were still pieces of him there—but you had to know where to look. Samuel walked over to the dressing table and opened the center drawer, which contained several boxes all neatly organized. Only one interested him; it was rectangular and covered in red velvet. He opened it. Inside was a gold dress watch that had belonged to his grandfather and then his father and was something his mother called an heirloom. One day the watch would be Samuel's, but until then, his mother kept it for herself.

From out in the hall, a floorboard creaked. Samuel froze, the watch nestled in his hand. He glanced at the door, held his breath, refused to swallow even though his throat was practically demanding it. Any noise was reckless at such a time. The boards made no further protest and the relief rippled through his body.

Samuel surrendered the watch, closed the box and returned it to the drawer. He walked silently around the bedroom. The boy looked at things, touched them, moved on, saw and touched the next thing, arriving at the chest of drawers. What a dull thing a chest of drawers was. It never held the great promise of a locked cupboard or a safe hidden behind a painting. With little enthusiasm, he pulled open the middle drawer and looked inside. It was as miserable as he expected—just a few pairs of stockings and undergarments, some old lace handkerchiefs and a photo album or two. He allowed a disappointed sigh. Then he opened the top drawer, which was littered with the gloves and scarfs his mother hadn't taken with her and a blanket that had been his father's when he was a baby.

The blanket's wool was frayed but soft, peach colored, with lambs and blue birds embroidered over it. Samuel placed his hand on it, just to feel its soft promise, but the blanket resisted his touch. Samuel lifted it up and discovered a tin hiding underneath. A tea tin. Naturally, such a discovery had to be investigated. He unscrewed the lid and found inside a pair of gold earrings, the very ones his mother was wearing in the photograph of his parents' wedding day on the bedside table, and a necklace with a sparkling red stone that his father gave to his mother when Samuel was born.

If finding them there puzzled him, the mystery was quickly solved. Hadn't his mother said once that only a chump leaves their best jewels in the dressing table or even a safe? Much smarter to hide them in an ordinary box just thrown in somewhere as if of no value or importance at all. The tin was nothing less than a confirmation of his mother's great wisdom. Samuel screwed the lid back on and placed the tin back where he found it. As he did, his hand brushed up against a small bulge in the last fold of the blanket. And there, tied with string, was a slim pile of letters.

Samuel sat down on the bed, untying the string. There were five letters in all, each one addressed to his father. Samuel recognized the handwriting right away. It was the same ornate scrawl that was on the postcards his mother had sent. These were her letters, sent to his father? Which raised so many questions and possibilities that Samuel was forced to stand up and then sit back down again. He opened the first letter with the fragile delicacy of a sacred scroll.

May 19, 1957
Dearest Vincent,

Yes, it was his mother writing to his father. The back of the envelope was an address in Somerset—a place called Lansdown in Bath—and the date was May of 1957. Samuel quickly deduced that this must have been when she was away resting. The letter had three pages and, unlike his postcards, the words were crammed tightly together as if his mother had a great deal to say. Her handwriting wasn't hard for him to understand as his teacher said he was a fine reader, better than almost everyone in the class except for Violet Winchester, even if he didn't have any regard for punctuation.

Samuel's eyes scanned down the first page and

then the second, flying over the blur of words and only stopping when his own name practically leaped out at him, as a person's own name will. Samuel. His mother was writing about him. Even though she had been far away in Bath, she must have been thinking of her boy. Why did that make him so happy? Of course she would be thinking of him. That's what mothers do when they're away from their children—they miss them dreadfully, a pain so awful it brings on fits of tears and heart shivers, and there's nothing that can fix it until they are reunited with their little ones. Samuel thought it best to scroll back to the previous sentence and start from there.

Please do come next weekend if you can, though I know how difficult things are at the factory. I would love to see you, my darling, but I think it would be better if you didn't bring Samuel. Dr. Boyle says it might

Samuel stopped reading. The trouble with a closed door is that there is always the possibility that someone will fling it open, especially when you are somewhere you aren't supposed to be. So a part of Samuel wasn't entirely surprised when he heard the door handle release its feeble squeak. He jumped off the bed and tucked the letters in the waist of his pants, covering them with his jumper as the door swung open. Ruth was there at the threshold, pale light flooding in around her.

"You're not to be in here," she said.

That was true. His mother never liked him being in her bedroom or the dressing room down the hall because these places were her sanctuary. Samuel was always getting under her feet, that's what she said, but surely his mother would have fallen down if he were under her feet? Which she never had, not once. Still, she needed time to herself. And he would always be tugging at her arm, begging her to play hide-and-seek or to go outside and watch him ride his bike or fly kites— but it wasn't fair to pester his mother because an afternoon of silly games could bring on a headache that lasted days. She wanted to play with him—there was no question about that—but his father had been better at that kind of thing, and besides, there was so much that needed her attention and a person only has two hands.

"What are you doing in this room, Samuel?" Ruth said.

"Nothing."

"Nothing?" Ruth walked into the bedroom as if she wasn't in any great hurry. "I find that very hard to believe."

"I just . . . I was thinking of Mother and missing her, so I came in here." Samuel tried his best to look as if he wasn't hiding something. "I wasn't doing anything wrong."

Ruth's lips pursed in condemnation. "So that's all you were up to? Standing in the middle of your mother's bedroom missing her?"

Samuel nodded.

"What's that under your jumper, Samuel?" Ruth said this soft and calm, which somehow made it worse. "Samuel, I asked you a question. What's under your jumper?"

The boy clenched his stomach as if the letters would magically sink into his skin and disappear. "Nothing."

"Nothing?" said Ruth for the second time.

"It isn't anything at all, Ruth. Like I said, I was missing—"

Her hand shot out, grabbing his jumper and yanking him toward her, while the other hand flew under his shirt and pulled the letters from his waist. She inspected the thin bundle. "Reading your mother's private letters is a wicked thing to do."

The boy said nothing.

"Is that what you've become, Samuel?" Ruth's once-soft voice crumbled under the familiar weight of her displeasure, heavy and full of sharp edges. "Is that what you are? A boy who sneaks about in bedrooms looking through drawers?"

"I just wanted to read them." He said this faintly.

"If it was meant for your eyes, your name would be on the envelope."

He didn't dare look up at her. "My name's inside, I saw it."

"Even more reason not to be reading it." Ruth cleared her throat. "You read every word, I suppose?"

Samuel shook his head. "Just a line or two."

"Yes, well . . ."

Ruth put the letters back in the drawer, closing it so hard it made the pictures on top rattle. Samuel stood rooted, unsure whether Ruth had reached the borderland of her anger yet. He heard her stalking back toward him, muttering something he couldn't catch, then her hand caught the crook of his arm, and she pulled him from the room.

"Deceitful, that's what you are," she said.

Out in the hallway she fished a set of keys from the pocket of her plain gray dress. "Just imagine it," she said, the crisp snap of the lock echoing through the corridor. "Having to lock Mrs. Clay's bedroom door so her own son won't sneak in and steal what doesn't belong to him."

It was the injustice that always bit hardest, sinking its teeth into him, making him say things that anyone with an ounce of common sense would keep to themselves. "What's so wrong with me reading Mother's letters? Did she say I couldn't? Father is gone, so he can't read them, and Mother told me I'm to have all that belonged to him and that must include those letters, too."

Ruth checked that the door was locked and

dropped the keys into her pocket. "Well said, Samuel, and quite right, too."

That wasn't what he had expected. Well said? Quite right? He looked up at her and saw from the stony look in her eyes, that unblinking stare, that she hadn't meant it at all. That she was making fun of him. Ruth released her hold on his arm in such a way that he stumbled, needing the wall to steady himself. She put her hand on his chest, pressing him against the oak panels. "Right is right and wrong is wrong and nothing you can say will make what you've done any less wicked. I expected better of you, Samuel Clay." She dropped her hand and smoothed down her dress. "Stay in your room until I call you for dinner. Is that clear?"

Samuel didn't answer, walking quickly to his bedroom and slamming the door. He half expected Ruth to come in and make a fuss again. But she didn't. If there were tears, he did his best to deny them. Ruth was a nasty beast who should be thrown down a well or locked in a dungeon. She didn't understand that he was only trying to be near her, that his mother was a creature in orbit and the one way he could feel close to her was to linger in the traces she left behind. All Ruth saw was the wrong he had done. That's all she ever saw. With a head full of sorrows, the only thing he could bear to do was stand by the window, arms folded, scowling out at the darkness. The night had rendered the garden an inky swamp and a part of him longed to dive into it and be gone. Mostly, though, he was thinking of his mother and those letters and what it all meant. Wondering where she was right now when he needed her most and willing her to come home to him.

6

He had all his meals in the kitchen with Ruth. It was easier that way and Ruth couldn't be expected to set a fine table morning and night for just one boy. Mostly they ate together, sitting opposite each other, talking about some little thing or other. But not always. When there was a chill between them, Ruth couldn't abide eating with the boy. She would wait until he was done, send him on his way and then take her meal.

Samuel didn't mind. Why would he want to eat with a rotten apple like Ruth Tupper, who wouldn't let him read those letters? Didn't he have every right to know what his mother said about him? How could he just go on with things when he knew there was a message from her locked away just across the hall from his bedroom? She hadn't wanted him to visit her in Bath. That's what she wrote. *It would be better if you didn't bring Samuel.* And that's what really sat under the frown on his face, whispering the question over and over. Why didn't she want him to visit?

"Are you eating that food or rearranging it?" Ruth put a glass of water in front of him.

Samuel looked down at the roast beef, potatoes and peas, the fork dangling from his fingers. "I don't like roast beef."

47

"Fine." Ruth picked up the plate and snatched the knife and fork from his hands. "Don't eat it, then."

"Give that back," said Samuel, and he didn't care that his voice was louder than Ruth would allow at the dinner table. "I said, give that back."

"Why would I do that? You don't like roast beef, remember?" She went to the scrap bin and dropped the contents of Samuel's dinner into it. "If you don't want what I've spent all afternoon cooking for you, well, I wouldn't dream of forcing it on you." She looked over at the boy and sniffed. "The same goes for those shortbread I set aside for your dessert."

"I'll tell Mother you threw my dinner away!" he shouted.

"Will you now?" Ruth sat herself down at the opposite end of the table and began filling her plate. "And will you also tell her what you were up to in her bedroom this afternoon?" She pierced a piece of beef with her fork and held it there. "I'm sure she'd want to know all about it—though I can only guess what she'd think of you then, Samuel."

"She would understand." But there was doubt in his voice and they both knew it. "Please, Ruth, let me see those letters. I promise I won't ever go into Mother's room again. I promise I won't, but Mother was writing about me and I just want to—"

"That subject is closed. You should be filled with remorse about what you did. Instead, you're boldly asking to invade your mother's privacy again. As if it's nothing at all." She was shaking her head now. "Shame on you."

The telephone began to ring out in the hall. Ruth looked toward the door, then back at Samuel. She said, "Don't move."

"I'll answer it," said Samuel, getting up.

Ruth stood, her finger pointed. "You'll do no such thing. Sit down."

She walked from the kitchen, her shoes clicking along the stone floor. They didn't get many phone calls at the house, not at night, anyway. Something was already stirring inside Samuel—right from that very first ring. It could be his mother calling or Uncle Felix, telling him that she had sent a telegram and that she was already sailing home. A phone ringing in the night was a promise, a promise of news. How could he sit there and wait?

The hall had a large chandelier, all crystal pendants and curved glass, but it wasn't burning and the lamps were switched off on account of economizing. What light there was spilled in from the kitchen with a little help from the half-moon outside, which cast the hall a foggy blue. Ruth was nearly at the phone when Samuel entered the hall. He was running by then. She

49

didn't turn to look at him, but Samuel was sure she must have heard him coming, because she quickened her steps, practically snatching the receiver just as he reached her.

"The Clay residence," said Ruth, slightly out of breath.

"Is it Mother?" asked Samuel.

Ruth shooed him away with her hand. "Good evening, Mrs. Harris."

Mrs. Harris. His mother's friend from the next village. She taught piano and every second Friday she read tea leaves and talked to spirits for anyone with fifty pence. Mrs. Harris had once sent word directly from Samuel's father, all the way from what she called "the other side." His mother didn't say what the message was but she came home all teary and said it sounded just like him. And now Mrs. Harris was on the telephone. Samuel couldn't have been more disheartened if he tried.

"I'm sorry, Mrs. Harris," Ruth was saying. "Mrs. Clay is still abroad . . . No, I don't have a firm date for her return, unfortunately."

"Has she heard from Mother?" said Samuel.

Ruth silently shushed him. "Yes, it was a sudden departure, but when the opportunity arose to meet with bankers in America, Mrs. Clay had little choice but to take it . . . No, it wasn't expected, Mrs. Harris, but then—"

Mrs. Harris seemed to have a lot to say, and the

whole time she was listening, Ruth played with the pin on the collar of her dress. It was silver with a four-leaf clover that sparkled with yellow stones, but Olive said they weren't even a tiny bit real and that Ruth treated that pin like the royal jewels because her father had given it to her.

"I don't know about that, Mrs. Harris." There was a lightness to Ruth's voice that hadn't been there before. "I'm sure Mrs. Clay is very busy. Last I heard she was in Boston . . . Well, no, she wouldn't be in meetings all day long." She laughed. "Yes, traveling the world does sound rather heavenly but, as I say, Mrs. Clay is not on a holiday." A pause. "Mrs. Harris, what a thing to say!"

Samuel couldn't explain why he had a knot in his stomach or why Ruth's laughter pulled on that knot until it was so tight he thought it might snap.

"Samuel?" said Ruth, glancing briefly at the boy. "He's well." Another pause. "Oh, yes, he keeps me on my toes. Actually, he's eating his dinner as we speak and I best get back to the kitchen while it's still standing." Laughter. "That's one way of putting it."

He didn't listen after that. His heart thumped in his chest and the anger was everywhere, seeping into his blood and rushing through his veins. Ruth had lied. She said lying was a terrible thing to do. But she lied. Lying and snickering with that old bat Mrs. Harris about his mother, making out she was having a wonderful time away from him.

Samuel didn't make the decision to strike out—suddenly, it was just happening. He bent his leg back and then swung it forward, striking her hard as he could in the shin. It only occurred to him later that it was almost exactly the same spot where he had been wounded just days before.

"Ah!" Ruth's cry made Samuel jump. What had he expected her to do but cry out? Pain flashed across her face and she took a breath with such force it sounded like a growl.

The boy ran then, bounding up the stairs. He stopped on the landing, squatting down, peering back at her through the wooden posts.

"No, Mrs. Harris, I'm . . . I'm fine." But her voice had a tight rasp to it. "Oh, nothing. I just . . . knocked my leg, is all." Her eyes flickered toward the landing but it was gloomy up there and Samuel hoped she couldn't see him. "Yes, I'm very clumsy. Forgive me, Mrs. Harris, but I must be going . . . Of course I'll let you know just as soon as I have word on Mrs. Clay's return. Good night."

Ruth hung up the phone and leaned on the side table for a moment or two with her eyes shut tight. Samuel heard her take a deep breath. Then she bent over, put a hand on her aching leg and cursed the devil.

7

Samuel didn't see Ruth again before bed. He had waited for her to come, but she never did. Nor did her footsteps echo down the corridor toward his room. It was as if she had disappeared.

Occasionally his eyes would leave the door and travel around the bedroom, glimpsing the picture of his mother holding him as a baby that sat on his bedside table or his collection of World War II fighter planes clustered along the window ledge or the wooden replica of the RMS *Queen Mary* sitting on the mantel or the painting of his father on a horse when he was just a boy, hanging above the fireplace.

Eventually his eyes grew heavy, but fears crowded in, demanding attention. He had kicked Ruth, hurt her; he'd never done that before. But in time even the very worst of his demons settled and the boy fell under sleep's spell.

He always slept deeply. So he never heard her boots on the wooden floors outside. Nor did he see her shadow under the door, nor did he hear the door open, gently. Light spilled into the room, though her silhouette carved out the best of it. The boy's back was to her but she saw the rise and fall of the blanket and heard his indolent breathing.

She walked toward the bed, favoring her left leg with an unmistakable limp. Still, her steps were not heavy and apart from the odd creek of a floorboard she was soon there, looking down. She bent forward, hands on her knees, and called the boy's name.

"Samuel," she said playfully. "Samuel."

The boy moved just a little but quickly settled again.

"Samuel." She said it louder this time but still full of good cheer. "Samuel, wake up. Your mother has come home."

The boy's eyes fluttered open but his mind was still a fog. He stretched and turned toward the voice, blinking into the darkness. "Mother's home?" Silence. "Ruth, is Mother—?"

He didn't see her hand draw back. He only felt the blow against his face, throwing his body sideways. He made a faint sound and the breath felt as if it were pulled from his body. Then that brief second or two when his skin tingled before the pain showed itself, spreading across his cheek like a flame. He shrank back, curling up into a ball and pulling the covers over him.

"You're dreaming, Samuel." Her voice practically sang. "Dreaming this whole thing."

Then she limped from the room, closing the door silently behind her.

8

Samuel stayed home from school the next day. Ruth said he had the makings of a cold, though he had barely coughed. Samuel knew the real reason but he didn't say it aloud. That's how it was with them. By morning the red had all but faded and his cheek didn't look any worse than what a short walk in a cold wind would do. It didn't hurt much. Not anymore.

"Have you made your bed?" Ruth was picking up his breakfast plate. As she walked to the sink, Samuel noticed she was limping slightly.

"No, Ruth."

Samuel's mother insisted that the boy always made his own bed. She said this was for his own good and that children who did nothing for themselves grew into impractical lumps. Normally, Samuel made it as soon as he got up, but not today. He had woken early, same as always, but this time his first thought wasn't about his mother. It was about her bedroom door. Her locked bedroom door. And how he might get into it.

As a general rule, Samuel always had a lot on his mind. So many thoughts and worries and troubles all bound up in the shape of his mother. But ever since he'd opened that letter, it was the only thing he could think about—though if he had stopped to consider it, this was bound up in the shape of her, too. His mother had written about him and told his father not to bring him down to Bath to visit her. Why? Why would she not want to see him? He had to know, that's all. So there was no other option than to read her words from start to finish.

Which is why he hadn't made his bed. He needed an excuse to go back upstairs and do the very thing he had been forbidden to do: break into his mother's bedroom and invade her privacy. Ruth said it was wrong but somehow it didn't feel anything but right. He simply had to read it. Now, that wasn't an easy matter, as Ruth kept the key in her possession. Last night, when Samuel was still hiding under the sheets, his cheek stinging, feeling nothing but mad at Ruth and wishing she would fall down the stairs or slip on some spilled porridge and break her neck, he remembered something. His mother kept a set of keys in her study. He had seen them many times when he was looking for this or that, and surely one of those keys would open her bedroom door? People always kept a spare key, didn't they?

"Well, then," said Ruth, taking the kettle off the stove, "as your bed won't make itself, I suggest you go and see to it. After that, you can do some work on that thing for Reverend Pryce. You're to write out a psalm and draw a picture, aren't you?"

"I left it at school."

"Well, start again. I'm sure there's a Bible in your mother's study." Ruth poured the hot water into the pot, clouds of steam rising around her like a mist. "Just because you're home from school doesn't mean you get to laze around like a dandy. What on earth are you gawking at?"

"Nothing."

"Nothing indeed. Then would you mind getting a move on?"

"Yes, Ruth." Samuel did his best not to look even slightly pleased as he hurried from the kitchen.

The keys were in the last drawer of the desk. There were three of them strung on a silver loop. One had an ornate design and Samuel recognized it as belonging to the study door, while the other two both were plain and looked very much like the key Ruth had used to lock his mother's bedroom. There was a chance. Hope was alive. It was a small win and he took it.

Samuel was hurrying toward his mother's bedroom, clutching the keys tightly so they didn't jangle. He'd just reached the door when he heard her.

"Are you making that bed?" she called from downstairs.

"Doing it now, Ruth."

"Playing with your planes more like it," she replied.

"I'm not," he called back, even in that moment unable to endure a false allegation.

Ruth may have huffed then or muttered something—he couldn't be sure. Nor did it matter. As carefully as he could, he slipped the first key in the lock, hoping against hope that it would open. It jammed as he turned it. So he tried the second key, even asking his father to please let this be the one. His father was in heaven watching over him or was sleeping for eternity; Samuel had heard conflicting information. But at that moment he needed all the help he could get.

Biting down on his bottom lip, he turned the key. It twisted with ease; the sound of the lock slipping back was as sweet as church bells. The boy passed inside and closed the door behind him. He moved quickly across the room and opened the top drawer, looking for the letters—they were under the tea tin, which was under the blanket. The tin rattled with the sound of his mother's earrings and necklace when he lifted it and in the quiet of the room it sounded like cannon fire.

"Samuel?" It was Ruth. Her footsteps now drumming the corridor outside.

The boy held his breath. Kept as still as he could manage, the letters clutched in one hand, the tea tin in the other. He heard Ruth pass by the door and he reasoned she was heading toward his bedroom. Moments later, he heard her coming his way again.

"I'm in no mood for games, Samuel Clay." He heard Ruth sigh then. "Bed unmade, clothes on the floor. No better than a vagabond."

The percussion of her footsteps slowed as she passed his mother's door. Then they stopped. A tremor slithered up Samuel's spine. His hands began to tremble. If she opened the door, that would be it. He'd be done for. His eyes were fixed on the door handle. He prayed to his father for help again, hoping he'd intercede. Then the click of Ruth's boots on the floorboards broke the silence. She was walking back toward the landing.

The boy let out a shallow breath. He thought better of taking all the letters. What if Ruth were to check? So he took just the top one that he had been reading the day before. Then he placed the parcel of letters at the bottom of the drawer and covered them with the tea tin and the baby blanket. Next, he wiped the perspiration from the top of his lip, thanked his father for the help and hurried out to make his bed.

9

Ruth didn't search for long. She retreated to the kitchen and Samuel heard her banging about in there as he came down the stairs, the letter folded in his pocket. He knew how out of sorts she got when she couldn't find him and he thought that might explain all the pots and pans getting pummeled. Still, he had made his bed and he would just tell Ruth that he was up in the attic looking for a box of his father's old toys. He'd done that before so it wouldn't sound unlikely.

Samuel practically ran to the study. He put the keys back where he found them and then searched the bookshelves for a Bible. He found one, a large volume with embossed gold lettering, which he'd never seen his mother or his father holding. Then he sat down at his mother's desk and opened the book, searching for Psalm 3—all about David, who was fleeing from his son Absalom—which is the one he had to write out for Reverend Pryce's school visit next week. Everything had to look just so should Ruth suddenly appear. Which she certainly would.

He retrieved the envelope from his pocket and took out the letter. His mother had numbered the pages in the top right-hand corner. There were three in all. So, he began.

May 19, 1957

Dearest Vincent,

I received your present yesterday and it was a lovely surprise. The scarf is beautiful and just the thing to wrap around me when I take my walks through town. I could write for days about the hot springs, though I fear that would bore you silly! Oh, but they really are something. The heat was a shock to begin with, I won't lie, but I have come to love it. I really believe the water and the vapors have great healing powers and my soul feels all the lighter for it. Heavens, I must sound ludicrous! But honestly, my darling, Bath is just as Dr. Boyle said, the ideal place to refresh myself.

The letter went on like this for the rest of the page, and as much as Samuel wanted to savor every one of his mother's words, he really only had one destination in mind: the next page, where he knew she had begun to talk about him. He read quickly, about how his mother was filling her days bathing in the hot springs and going for long walks and something she called *sessions* with a Dr. Boyle. Samuel didn't know why she would need a doctor when all she was doing was resting, but he decided that perhaps a doctor was just the thing with all that hot water and vapors.

I can breathe here and think clearly just like my old self. Does that make me sound horribly selfish? I do try to be all that I am supposed to be, I hope you know that, but it is very hard. I want to be better when I come home, better for all of us. At the moment, however, I do not feel ready, which makes me feel like a heel. I know how much all this is costing and that it is money we don't have.

Please do come next weekend if you can, though I know how difficult things are at the factory. I would love to see you, my darling, but I think it would be better if you didn't bring Samuel. Dr. Boyle says it might set me back.

He also says that I must be honest with you and so I will. When you write and tell me how much Samuel misses me and how he cries for me, it only makes things worse. If you only knew how wretched I feel when he is

"Samuel, are you in the study?" Ruth's voice swept in from the great hall and the boy was suddenly aware that she was walking toward the study.

"Yes, Ruth." Samuel folded the letter and slipped it between the pages of the Bible.

She entered the room with her hands already on her hips. "Just where were you when I was calling all over the house?"

Samuel told her about being in the attic. As he did, he tried hard not to look down at the Bible. Ruth noticed things like that.

"The attic?" Ruth scowled like she hadn't considered that. "I suppose you've dragged more clutter down for me to dust?"

The boy shrugged. "I didn't find anything worth playing with."

"Is that so?" Ruth let her hands drop down as she walked toward Samuel. "Up in the attic with all those treasures, old boats and toy soldiers, and you come down empty-handed?"

Samuel nodded, glancing down at the Bible without meaning to.

Ruth gazed at him for a very long time. She sniffed and said, "Didn't I tell you to make your bed?"

"It's done." He looked up at her. "I'm sorry I didn't come when you were calling, I didn't hear you up in the attic, that's all."

Ruth sniffed again. She always seemed on the brink of a cold. "Yes, well, I need you to fetch some wood for the stove. William left it outside the kitchen. I'm in the middle of making a mince pie and there's hardly a twig left to burn."

"Yes, Ruth." Samuel closed the book and managed to look bored. "Anything's better than reading the Bible."

"What a thing to say." Ruth was walking about the study now. "I confess, I'm more than a little surprised that you're in here actually doing as you were told. A minor miracle, surely?"

"I've nothing else to do." Samuel looked out the window for good effect. "Could I play outside once I bring in the wood?"

"You've got a cold, remember?" Ruth was playing with the clover pin on her collar. "Are you feeling better, then?"

Samuel nodded.

"Good."

Sometimes Samuel would wonder about Ruth—where she was from and such. He didn't know much about her, only what he'd heard from his parents or Olive. There had been some talk of a sweetheart, that's what Olive said, but the war had taken him. Or he had come back but wasn't the same. Either way, nobody believed that Ruth had ever married. When Samuel's parents talked about Ruth they seemed to find it funny that there hadn't been any admirers calling at the house, no letters from distant shores, that perhaps something in her manner—the stiffness of her posture, the relentless buckle of her brow—

suggested a certain exasperation. That was his father's word. Or was it disappointment? his mother had asked.

Ruth was from up north. At least, Samuel thought she was. One day as lunch was being served, Samuel's mother had asked about her family. Ruth said her sister was all she had left and the rest of her kin were long buried. His mother had frowned then, put down her napkin and inquired about Ruth's hopes. She couldn't imagine a life without the possibility of brighter days. Surely Ruth had dreams? Something she was counting on or hoping for? Did she want to open a teashop or write a novel or visit the pyramids? Ruth just blushed and said she had all she needed right there with them. When she left the room to fetch more coffee, Samuel's mother said that Ruth wasn't being honest. She cared about something enough to keep it to herself. That blush was as good as saying it aloud.

"While I applaud your sudden dedication, Samuel, I need that wood before my pie turns into a holy disaster," Ruth said, patting down her hair and checking the tightness of her bun. "You can go on with your schoolwork after lunch."

"Yes, Ruth."

Samuel stood up and, as he did, Ruth leaned over the desk and picked up the Bible. "I'd be more comfortable if you worked out in the kitchen," she said. "That way I'll know you're doing more than daydreaming."

"I can carry it," said Samuel, passing quickly around the desk.

Ruth glanced down at the Bible. "Suit yourself."

She handed the book to Samuel. The boy hugged it close to his chest and followed her out.

Before fetching the firewood, Samuel went to the kitchen garden looking for his rabbit. It wasn't technically his rabbit, being wild and unruly, but as there weren't any competing claims of ownership, Samuel didn't think there was any harm in assuming custody. The creature was rather elusive, but most days he could be counted on to make a fleeting appearance near the row of thriving cabbages. Though today there was no sign of him, which the boy took as a personal slight.

After he brought the firewood in, Ruth made Samuel work for over an hour writing out the psalm—and he still wasn't even half-done. For her part, the housekeeper finished the mince pie and then prepared a small side of pork for dinner. But her focus, amid all of this activity, remained fixed on the boy. She would stop on her way from the oven to the larder or the table to the cupboards, glancing over Samuel's shoulder, telling him to slow down or lift his head or offering one disparaging comment or another about the state of his handwriting. All the while Samuel thought of what was hidden between the pages of the Bible, scared silly that she might find it there.

When the pork was roasting in the oven, Ruth asked Samuel to help her bring the washing in. As Samuel stood, Ruth, with flawless speed, scooped up the Bible.

"I wasn't finished," he said.

"While I admire your enthusiasm, though it's *wildly* out of character . . ." Ruth smiled faintly then. "You can finish it tomorrow after school."

She set the Bible on a table by the icebox.

Later that night, after he had gotten ready for bed and brushed his teeth, Samuel stole down the back stairs and into the kitchen, praying the letter would still be there and that Ruth hadn't found it. She hadn't and the relief was as glorious as it was instant.

With the letter in hand, the boy tore across the great hall and into his mother's study, where he hid the folded pages in the back of the atlas somewhere around the Antarctic.

Samuel could have taken the letter to his bedroom and read it by lamplight. But for some reason he didn't choose to, not right away. The letter had left him feeling out of sorts; there was no denying that. While the words were his mother's and in one way it sounded just like her, in other ways, it was the voice of someone else entirely. And he knew whose—that horrid Dr. Boyle. He was the one who had persuaded his mother that a visit from Samuel would *set her back*. What did that mean? He wouldn't have been more than five years old then. Was he so very naughty that his mother had to be warned not to have him close? Yes, the letter had left him out of sorts and it would take some thinking about. For without knowing exactly why, Samuel felt in the deepest part of himself that to read any further might lead him into waters deeper than he could tread.

10

Though it was autumn, the Cornish oak seemed unwilling to release any of its bounty. Samuel thought this reflected poorly on the tree and hinted at a lack of generosity. One of his favorite games—he and Joseph played it at least twice every week—was to stand under the tree and catch the falling leaves. They weren't just falling leaves, though; each one was weighted with momentous consequence. Catch this leaf and you will sleep peacefully that night; let it slip through your fingers and you will die before you wake. Clutch that one in your hand and you'll play cricket for England; if you miss and it reaches the ground, you'll be blinded on the spot.

Ruth had sent him outside to pull some carrots for dinner but somehow he had found his way under the oak tree. It was true, the game wasn't as much fun without Joseph there—his consequences were always far more ghoulish than anything Samuel could think up—but even a dull game of "catch the leaf" was better than pulling carrots.

Samuel looked up and the tree seemed to heave, the sunlight ricocheting through the web of branches. He felt the breeze pick up over the hilltop, and a leaf dropped from high up. It flipped several times, the wind curving its belly as it swayed in great sweeps.

Samuel quickly decided the stakes. If he caught the leaf, his mother would be home by week's end. If he didn't, then she was never coming back. The boy's head was tilted back, his arms stretched up above his head, his eyes trained only on the leaf. He stumbled over one of the roots, though quickly found his footing. His hopes soared as the leaf, now a green smudge bound up in his greatest wish and deepest fear, spiraled down. Samuel jumped at just the right moment, but then the breeze seemed to wake again from its slumber, collecting the leaf and carrying it far from his grasp, down into the tall grass.

Though it was just a leaf and there were sure to be many others, it was a blow, and being a boy who felt that fate had a hand in the breaking of a pencil or the spilling of a drink, he couldn't help but think that he had failed and that his mother would suffer for it.

The carrots couldn't be avoided forever so that's where he went. There was a welcome consolation, though, huddled under the hedge, which ran along the far side of the kitchen garden. The rabbit shifted on its back legs and sniffed the air when Samuel drew near—which was as close to a friendly greeting as he ever offered. It wasn't an especially attractive animal, a muddy-brown coat with the hint of ginger. But the eyes glistened as if they had a secret and the rabbit always seemed preoccupied, even busy, which Samuel found deeply impressive. Naturally, he had wanted to make things more permanent but his mother couldn't abide a cage of any kind, even a spacious hutch. Though she did help him select a name. Samuel was keen on Blink since the rabbit did this incessantly, but his mother said this focused on a shortcoming, which was typical of an English child, and not to be countenanced. Couldn't Samuel focus on the rabbit's strengths instead? A few inadequate names were thrown around, until they arrived at Robin Hood. It was his mother's suggestion and her reasons were sound. She said that Robin Hood had lived in the wild and did as he pleased, just like the rabbit, and that such a life was to be admired.

"It's me," said the boy as softly as he could. The rabbit jumped when Samuel crouched down and reached out his hand. Robin Hood had no tolerance for being petted, though he would submit to Samuel's company for a cabbage leaf or, in a pinch, a piece of apple. "Hungry?"

Of course the rabbit was hungry. Wasn't he staring with great intensity at the row of cabbages covered in wire? The wire was Ruth's idea. She had nothing good to say about Robin Hood and thought it foolhardy of Samuel's mother to let the boy feed it. She said no good could come of such an indulgence and her greens would pay the price.

Lifting the edge of the wire, Samuel tore off a corner of cabbage and held it out. The offer was quickly accepted and the green leaf devoured as if it were a last meal. Having gotten what he came for, the rabbit turned its back and was gone.

Samuel sighed and walked slowly to the carrots, pulling five or six from the ground, none of them especially big, and threw them into the basket. It didn't take long. When Samuel set off for the house, he saw Ruth at the back door. She was talking to someone, and although that person had their back to Samuel, he knew right away that it was Olive. She was short and plump, hunched over, her plaited blond hair in a knot. She was barely nineteen, but Samuel's mother once said she had the bearing of a middle-aged washerwoman. Whatever that meant.

Ruth was holding something in her hand—it looked like a letter—and she was waving it around with a stern look on her face. Whatever they were talking about, Samuel wanted no part of it, so he left the basket at his feet and went to find his bike.

As he flew down the drive, the wheels churning over the gravel, he almost forgot how everything was wrong, and when he neared the front gates, Samuel surrendered to his reckless soul and squeezed the brakes as hard as he could. The tires seized up and began to slide, the bike spinning in an exhilarating half circle, stirring up the gravel and shooting it through the air. He put a foot down to steady the bike and allowed a faint smile—at least something had gone right that day. This feeling didn't sit inside him long. For coming down the drive, wiping her eyes and hugging her pale blue coat, was Olive.

When she saw Samuel, Olive sniffed and said, "I must look a state."

Samuel made no reply.

"I was hoping Ruth might be able to keep me on, even just a half day a week. I told her I'd work for less—anything's better than nothing, don't you think? But Ruth said no—didn't even let me finish what I was saying. Just no." Olive unspooled her arms and Samuel saw that she was holding a letter. "She gave me a reference, which is something, I suppose. There's a position going up at Braddon Hall, so I'll try there but . . . there's other girls with more experience." Olive hugged herself again. "My ma can't work much anymore—her knees are awful bad—so I have to find something or else . . ."

"Or else what?" Samuel asked.

"Well, we won't eat, that's what."

"We have food here. There's always plenty of leftovers and the garden is full of vegetables, though the carrots are small."

For some reason this made Olive's lips tremble. "Sorry," she said.

Samuel didn't know what for.

Then Olive looked at Samuel as if she might be waiting for him to say something. When he didn't, she said, "Does Ruth . . . What I mean is, do you like living here with her?"

"I live with Mother."

" 'Course you do, but when she's away, I mean. I know Ruth's as strict as they come, but does she treat you well?"

Samuel was playing with the brakes on his bike. "Yes."

"The other morning, when you hurt yourself in the kitchen, cut your leg, remember?"

The boy nodded.

"Did it really happen like you said?" Olive was staring now. "Or did Ruth do something to make you fall?"

"I tripped, that's all."

She sighed. "I'm pleased to hear it. I was just worried."

"What were you worried about?"

"Doesn't matter." She tapped his nose. "You take care, okay?"

When Samuel brought the basket of carrots into the kitchen, Ruth told him to take his shoes off at the back door because she had spent all morning scrubbing the kitchen floor and it was backbreaking work and it would be just about the last straw if Samuel ran dirt and grass across it. Samuel was sitting on the step, doing as he was told, when Ruth said, "I saw you talking to Olive by the gate."

"She was crying," Samuel said.

"Too emotional for her own good, that girl."

"Her mother can't work and Olive is worried about eating."

Ruth picked up the basket of carrots at Samuel's feet. "I can't very well keep her on without the money to pay her, now can I?"

Samuel placed his shoes under the window and then went into the kitchen, where Ruth was boiling a cabbage—its rank perfume filled the room, making the boy frown. "Olive said she might get a job at the hall."

"It's possible, but I wouldn't think so." Ruth sounded sure. "Did Olive say anything else?"

Samuel shook his head.

"You were down there for quite some time." Ruth was staring at him just like Olive had. "She didn't say anything else? Nothing at all?"

"No, nothing."

Ruth smoothed down her apron and didn't look at all content. "Well, come in and wash your hands, then you can help me peel these carrots."

"How long's it been now?"

"Sixteen and a half weeks," said Samuel, panting. "One hundred and seventeen days."

"Not one telegram?" said Joseph, leaning against the front gate.

"Just postcards." Samuel pushed the hair from his eyes. "Eight of them."

The two boys were outside Samuel's front gate, having run all the way up the hill, their bags and hats in puddles at their feet. Every Wednesday after school Joseph was allowed to come over for shortbread and hot chocolate. Ruth didn't allow Samuel to visit Joseph's house for reasons she didn't think it proper to mention.

"And you don't even know where she's staying in Boston?" said Joseph. "That's rotten."

"She's very busy meeting with important people."

Joseph spat. "What's so important about them?"

Samuel shrugged, still out of breath. "They have money."

"And you don't." When Samuel looked at Joseph funny, the boy said, "My dad works with Olive's uncle and he said she's been let go. He told my dad there's no money left to pay her wages."

"Mother's going to fix everything. That's why she's away."

"Thing is," said Joseph, picking up his school bag and slinging it over his shoulder, "I know she didn't say goodbye or anything, but you're the lucky one, seems to me."

Samuel collected his own bag and put on his hat. "Why?"

Samuel and Joseph were exactly the same height, which at times seemed to be the very foundation of their friendship. They measured themselves at the end of every week, equally pleased when the numbers came in and they were still growing at the same rate. But that was where the physical similarities ended. While Samuel had his mother's slight build, her dark hair, pale skin and green eyes, Joseph was a different proposition altogether—stocky, with sandy hair, a large round face and a bounty of freckles.

"Well," said Joseph, shoving his school cap into his pocket, "I reckon I'd give just about anything to have my mum disappear for one hundred and seventeen days."

They passed through the gates and walked up the drive.

"She hasn't disappeared." Samuel was frowning. "She's in America."

"I never said she wasn't." Joseph bumped the other boy's shoulder to take the sting out. "Look, all I'm saying is, at least you don't have your mum shouting at you to wipe your feet or take a bath. You can do anything you want."

Samuel shook his head. "Not with Ruth around."

"Oh, yeah, forgot about her."

Samuel went to say something but stopped himself. Then he said, "She doesn't let me answer the telephone."

"Why not?"

"I don't know. Mother always lets me."

"She can't tell you what to do." Joseph spoke

with complete authority. "It's your mother who pays her, and when you think about it, that has to make you her master, as well."

"No one tells Ruth what to do."

Joseph wiped his nose. "She's just a house-keeper, you know. My mum gets an awful time cooking for those toffs up at the hall. Even the little ones bark orders at her."

"Mother says that when she's away, Ruth's in charge."

"She's always away."

Joseph didn't say this to be cruel, which somehow made it worse.

"She'll be home soon," said Samuel. "Any day now, that's what Ruth says."

It wasn't true, but what choice did he have? They were at the front door by now and the hot afternoon sun fell away as they passed under the portico. Samuel had his hand on the doorknob when Joseph stopped him.

"Don't get mad, but my mum says it's strange, your mum leaving all of a sudden like she did." The boy's booming voice had faded to a conspiratorial whisper. "She says it's like she ran off or something."

That was too much for Samuel to take. He didn't mean to push his friend but that's what he did. "She didn't run away." He pushed him again. "Take that back!"

"Don't blame me, I didn't say it." Then Joseph

gasped—he hardly ever gasped—and his eyes seemed to swell with dark wonder. "Bloody hell."

Samuel didn't want to ask but there was no getting around it. "What?"

"I heard about this housekeeper—"

The front door swung open and Ruth was there, eyeing both boys with considerable suspicion. "Who's yelling loud enough to wake the dead?"

"No one, Ruth," said Samuel.

Joseph flashed a smile. "We were just talking about your delicious shortbread."

Ruth didn't look convinced. "Well, unless you want to eat them out there on the drive, I suggest you come in." She pointed at Joseph in an accusing fashion. "And take that school hat out of your pocket, Joseph Collins, and put it neatly with your bag by the door."

Samuel watched as Joseph did just what he was told.

"You, too," said Ruth, looking at Samuel.

"Did you hear from Mother, Ruth?" Samuel put down his bag and took off his cap. "Did she send a telegram? Did she—?"

"Not today." Ruth was already walking from the hall. "Wash your hands, then come into the kitchen," she instructed. "If you promise not to make a mess, you can have your afternoon tea in Samuel's room. I know you'll be wanting those blessed planes and I won't have you stampeding up and down the stairs like madmen."

When Ruth was safely out of earshot, Samuel turned to Joseph and said, "What were you going to say?"

"About what?"

"How should I know? You were saying something and then you swore and then—"

"Oh, that. Tell you later." Joseph pointed at Ruth, who was nearly at the kitchen door. "Why's she limping?"

Samuel dug his hands into his pockets. "Must have fallen or something."

"Clumsy, is she?"

Samuel ignored the question and instead raised the promise of shortbread and hot chocolate, once they were washed up. It worked like a charm and moments later the boys were in a race to the bathroom.

11

Planes and soldiers were scattered across the room like the remnants of a bloody skirmish. Each boy sat cross-legged on the bed with a plate in his lap containing two shortbreads.

"Careful, it's hot." Ruth set the cups of hot chocolate down on the bedside table. "And not a crumb on that bed or there will be a fuss made."

"Yes, Ruth," said Samuel.

"We'll be careful," promised Joseph, unable to resist the biscuits a moment longer.

Ruth patted down her hair and looked only at Samuel. "Mind you are."

As she walked from the bedroom, she reminded Joseph that his mother expected him home by four thirty and that the poor woman had enough to contend with—Samuel didn't know what— without the boy being tardy.

When her footsteps were safely fading down the corridor, Joseph felt it was the perfect moment to say, "She's a dragon, that one."

But Samuel didn't care about that or biscuits or crumbs. Joseph had a story and for reasons he couldn't explain, even to himself, Samuel wanted to hear it. "Tell me what you were going to say."

Joseph's mouth was full at the time and all he managed to say was, "Hold on."

He put down his plate and got up, walking across the room and peering down the hall. Then he closed the door, picking up a cup of hot chocolate on his way back. "When we were talking before—about your mum being away and how she went in the night while you were sleeping and all—I remembered something."

Samuel hoped it was some news about his mother, though he couldn't imagine how Joseph could have any. Still, he leaned forward. "What did you remember?"

"Well . . ." Joseph glanced at the door for good effect, his voice falling to a hush. "My mum was talking with Lady Margaret from the hall and she told her about this housekeeper who worked for a family in Germany." He scrunched up his freckled nose. "Or was it Italy?"

"Is it important?" said Samuel.

"Suppose not. Anyway, this housekeeper was pleasant enough and kept the house sparkling clean, but underneath all that she was bonkers. Mad as a hatter. But the nice family she worked for didn't know it, did they?"

Samuel was listening so intently the plate had slipped from his lap.

"One night," continued Joseph, sipping his hot chocolate, "while the family was sleeping, all peaceful in their beds, the housekeeper crept into their rooms. Now you've got to understand something—this housekeeper was a great fat thing, but she didn't make one little sound she was so quiet."

Samuel's eyebrows had lifted. "What did she do?"

Joseph set down the hot chocolate and moved closer to Samuel. "She crept into their bedrooms, just like I said, quiet as a mouse, and she walked right up to where they were sleeping and then she . . ."

The pause was intolerable. "What? What did she do?"

Joseph lunged, grabbing Samuel by the shoulders. "She cut their throats!"

Samuel jumped when Joseph grabbed him, which was shameful. "You're lying," he said, wriggling free. "I know you're lying, Joseph."

The grin faded from the boy's lips. "It's no lie, Samuel. It happened just like I said—that's how Lady Margaret told it to my mum, anyway." He took a bite of shortbread. "And that's not all, either. After the housekeeper murdered the whole family, she dragged their bodies down to the cellar, then she burned all the blood-soaked sheets to get rid of the evidence and the next day she told the neighbors that the family had gone abroad all of a sudden."

"Why . . . why would the housekeeper do that?"

"Why do you think?" Joseph wiped his nose. "She got to live like Lady Muck in their fine house, not having to pick up after them, make

83

their dinners, wash their clothes. For six months she carried on like nothing was wrong, like the family were having a great old time in South America or somewhere."

"And then?" said Samuel.

Joseph shrugged. "Then some friends of the family got all suspicious and called the coppers and they searched the house and found the mother and father and all the little ones rotting in the cellar."

"I don't understand." Samuel spoke softly. "She must have known she'd get found out eventually. She must have known she would hang for it."

"Like I said, she was bonkers." Joseph was firm on this. "Some people just are—no one knows why."

The threads of this story had begun to fix themselves around Samuel, as the right story will often do, and the harder he willed himself to resist it, the tighter the yarn pulled. "I don't see what that's got to do with me. It's just a stupid story."

"Maybe you're right." Joseph was now hard at work on the second shortbread. "But think about it, Samuel. Your mum goes away in the dead of night, all of a sudden, no warning, no goodbyes. And the only person to see her go was Ruth."

"It was late . . . I was asleep."

"That's another thing—who decides to travel across the world late one night?" Joseph burped. "Sounds fishy to me."

The threads twisted and Samuel swallowed hard. "Why wouldn't Ruth have killed me, too?"

"That's easy. She needed to keep you around so no one would get suspicious."

"Ruth loves Mother—they are great friends."

"Even great friends come to blows, Samuel," said Joseph, picking up a World War II bomber from the bed. "What if your mum was going to have to let Ruth go, just like Olive, because she'd run out of money and she couldn't pay her wages." Joseph's voice lifted as he fell under the spell of his own gruesome theory. "She tells Ruth, 'You're fired, you have to go,' and they argue because Ruth doesn't have anywhere to go and she's wasted all her good years working for you lot. Things get heated and she hits your mum. Maybe she didn't mean to do it so hard, but she does and then it's too late. So she cleans everything up, blood and all, and puts Mrs. Clay down in the cellar before you wake up."

"No." Samuel was shaking his head. "Ruth wouldn't do anything like that."

"What proof do you have that your mum is really in America?" Joseph crashed the plane into the pillow, simulating an explosion. "You said she hasn't sent any telegrams."

"She sends postcards. She writes to me."

"Ruth might have a friend in America who's sending them," suggested Joseph with a shrug.

"I know her handwriting. It's Mother."

Joseph leaned back against the iron bed frame with his hands behind his head. "You're probably right." He said this cheerfully. "A person would need an awful bad temper to kill someone in cold blood. I know she's tough as old boots, but Ruth doesn't seem the violent type. Too prim and proper."

Samuel didn't say anything. His heart was a drumbeat in his chest.

"I wouldn't worry about it, Samuel." Joseph had a talent for upsetting people, usually just by opening his mouth and letting whatever he was thinking spill out, but he knew he had taken things too far. "That story . . . I was just trying to scare you." Joseph nudged the boy playfully. "It's like you said—your mum will be home any day now. She'll probably have a trunk full of presents and all."

Samuel nodded.

"It's just a story, Samuel. It doesn't mean anything."

Samuel shifted his gaze, finding his friend and offering him the smile he was waiting on. "I know."

12

The flashlight peeled away the darkness clinging to the kitchen. The narrow beam moved quickly, flying up the wall and down the cupboards, finally spotlighting the stone floor in an apricot haze. Samuel stood in the doorway, dressed in his pajamas, his feet bare, letting the flashlight do the traveling for him. He didn't dare turn on the light. For the longest time he didn't even move.

The boy had always been afraid of the dark—it seemed a perfectly sensible thing to be. How could you not be afraid of a great veil of shadows that could hide anything in its embrace? But the darkness didn't explain why he was rooted to the spot. This time it was the light that scared him most.

So he stood there peering into the empty kitchen, willing his legs to move. He had to know, that's all. He hadn't thought of anything else since Joseph went home. The story about the housekeeper who had murdered the family she worked for and hid their bodies in the cellar was fixed in his thoughts, crowding out everything else. Yes, Joseph said it was just a story and didn't mean anything, but sometimes a person hears a thing and it binds itself around you so tightly that there's no ignoring it.

The worst part was that it made sense. The family vanishing in the night. The only witness, the trusted housekeeper. Didn't it all fit?

Ruth was the only one to see his mother leave. She told everyone his mother was abroad while she ran the house as if it were her own. Yes, there were loose threads—the postcards, for one. And the fact that she hadn't killed him, as well. But Ruth had done something bad, he was sure of that. She had done something to his mother, his beautiful mother, who wanted nothing more than to be with him and take care of him and love him like only a mother can. He was her little man and it made a horrible kind of sense that it would take something beastly, something awful that Ruth had done, to keep her away from him for one hundred and seventeen days.

All afternoon, doing his homework at the kitchen table and then eating dinner that night, he had thought on it as Ruth rushed about, picking things up and putting them down, telling him what to do and talking on about school and his hair needing a wash and his nails being in a sorry state. His eyes followed her every time she went into the larder to fetch something, knowing the door to the cellar was in there.

When Ruth complained that she had only two potatoes to boil for dinner, Samuel had jumped up. "I'll fetch you some."

He was nearly at the larder when Ruth stopped

him. "Just where do you think you're going?"

"To fetch you some more potatoes," said Samuel. "From the cellar."

"I've never seen you so eager to help."

The boy had no answer for that, but he tried. "I'm starving and you know how I like lots of potatoes when you roast a chicken." He turned toward the larder. "It will only take a second."

"Don't bother." Ruth was wiping her hands on a tea towel. "You won't find any down there. I'll pick some up when I take the shortbread to the market on Saturday." She gave Samuel a look then, like he wasn't making sense to her. "Back to your homework, please."

Once Ruth had sent him off to bed, he had stayed awake, listening for the sound of her coming up the stairs. She usually retired around nine o'clock, though he knew she never went straight to sleep. Sometimes Samuel would hear her moving about in her room long into the night, doing what he didn't know. Just a few minutes after nine, Samuel heard Ruth in the hall and then the sound of her bedroom door opening and closing. The boy waited another twenty minutes, just to be sure, before getting out of bed. He went to the wardrobe and took out the flashlight that had belonged to his father, then stole downstairs as quietly as he could manage.

Now here he was, standing at the kitchen

door, wondering if his mother was rotting down in the cellar. He closed his eyes for a moment. Brave, he needed to be brave. Not for himself, that wasn't it, but for her. Samuel's first steps were slow and wary as if he was uncertain of the ground underfoot. The beam of light flew out in front of him and he felt the cold stone floor and heard the hum and rattle of the icebox.

Despite his slow approach, Samuel soon found himself at the larder door. He shone the flashlight inside, illuminating the wooden shelves stocked with jars of pickles and sugar and flour and baskets of fruit and cabbages and carrots and bottles of treacle and vinegar. The narrow room held the fragrance of all these things, but mostly onions.

The flashlight's beam seemed to have a mind of its own and was soon gliding over the closed door at the end of the larder. It was made up of vertical boards, the gray paint peeling and the doorknob dented. Samuel walked toward it—he had a job to do, after all—aware of the sick feeling in the pit of his stomach and the cold clamminess of his hands and the dryness in his throat.

A person would need an awful bad temper to kill someone in cold blood. That's what Joseph said. Was Ruth a killer? Samuel knew her temper was short. He knew that she could lash out, be violent. But killing? Perhaps Ruth had merely kidnapped his mother. Yes, surely that was it.

They had argued, just like Joseph said, about Ruth being let go and the housekeeper had hit his mother, knocking her out. She panicked then, hiding his mother in the cellar, and she was down there right now. She would be hungry and sickly, but nothing that couldn't be fixed, and she would cry when she saw Samuel, joyful tears, because of all the people in the world he was the only one who had come to find her.

He pressed his hand to the door. Then he bent his head against the boards and closed his eyes. He made a sound then, little more than a faint groan, all the while thinking of her and wondering if it might really be true. He heard himself say her name, and his fingers slid down the door and found the handle.

Though his eyes were closed, the light flew at him.

"What on earth are you doing, child?"

The boy spun around. Ruth was standing at the mouth of the larder, her wavy brown hair loose around her shoulders, her nightdress concealed by a red robe, her finger still on the light switch. Though it was only a dim bulb, the room seemed lit up by a blinding sun.

"I asked you a question, Samuel." Ruth's voice took some account of the late hour and it sounded to Samuel like the words were a struggle, taking longer for her to say. "What are you doing down here at this hour of the night?"

"I . . . wanted something."

Ruth was moving toward him and Samuel stepped back, hitting the cellar door.

"Down here?" She looked at the flashlight in his hand. "What in heaven's name could you want at this hour? Were you hungry?"

There was an offering here—an easy way out—but Samuel couldn't take it. He pictured his mother in the cellar and it seemed to chase some of the fear from his voice. "I wasn't hungry. I wanted to see."

"See what?" Ruth was standing over him now and Samuel smelled the sourness of her breath. "See what, Samuel?"

The boy turned and looked at the cellar door. "I wanted to see something down there."

"Down in the cellar?"

Samuel nodded.

"What on earth could you want down there?"

"Father's things." He had intended to be truthful, but with Ruth glaring down at you, courage was hard to find. "His toys from when he was a boy."

"You know very well your father's old toys are in the attic. What has come over you?" Ruth put her hand on his forehead. "Are you feeling ill?" Then she grabbed Samuel by the arm. "Come, let's get you back to bed. We'll talk about this in the morning."

Samuel pulled away, the anger smothering his

fear. "I want to see what's in the cellar right now."

"You'll do no such thing. I won't have you going down there in the dead of night and breaking your neck."

"I will see it!" he shouted. "I will go down there!"

He turned and grabbed the handle, pushing on the door.

"It's locked." Ruth sounded calm. "You're being ridiculous, Samuel."

Samuel turned back to face her. "Give me the key."

"I will not."

"Give me the key, Ruth!"

Ruth raised her finger and moved it between his eyes. "You hush your voice. It's late, and it's plain to see you're not well, so I'm going to overlook this boldness. But you can forget about going down to the cellar. It's a great mess and, like I said, you'd probably break your neck."

"I don't care, I want to see."

"There's nothing down there." Ruth dropped her hand. "Just a stack of damp, moldy boxes, some old wine and a lot of big, ugly rats."

"Why is the door locked?"

"Well . . . it always has been locked, for as long as I've been here, anyhow. Cellars are locked, that's all there is to it."

Samuel shook his head. "I'm not leaving until I see."

She sprang then, grabbing him by the shoulders with such force the flashlight dropped from his hand. "See what, child? There's nothing down there, I just told you, nothing that you'd care to look at, anyhow."

The dread rose up from the pit of his stomach and had nowhere to go, so the tears gathered and fell, his voice hardly a whisper. "What did you do, Ruth?"

He pushed her with all of his might and ran from the larder.

13

There was nowhere else to go but bed so that was where he went. He lay on his back, the blanket pulled up around his chin. It was pitch-dark but he didn't mind because somehow it made things easier. He hadn't cried so hard in a long time. It was all about his mother and the cellar. And of course there was fear there, too. Ruth was cruel and hateful and she had it in her to hurt someone. Even kill them? Yes, he thought so.

Why was the cellar door locked? If she had nothing to hide, why wouldn't she let him go down and see? Samuel was so lost in the burden of his troubles that he didn't hear Ruth approaching. Not until the door opened and she was coming toward him. He knew that pulling the blanket over his head was a stupid thing to do, something you might expect from an infant, not a nine-year-old boy, but that's what he did.

He heard the lamp being switched on and felt the bed shift as she sat down.

"May I see you? Come now, you'll suffocate under there."

"Go away."

When Samuel didn't lower the blanket, Ruth's fingers curled around the covers and, in her own firm way, forced them below the boy's eyes.

"Much better." She pushed the hair from Samuel's forehead and her touch was surprisingly tender. "What is making you cry so? Tell me what's the matter and I'll try my best to fix it."

"Where is my mother?"

"Oh, Samuel, you know where she is. She's in America trying to—"

"I don't believe you."

"Well, I'm sorry to hear that."

Samuel thought she sounded more cross than sorry.

"You've worked yourself into a terrible state over heaven knows what," she said. "Why would I lie about where your mother is?"

The boy lowered the blanket just under his chin and though he couldn't look at Ruth—that was asking too much—the words found their way out. "Because you killed her."

"Killed her?" Ruth let out a gasp, which turned into a faint chuckle. "Well, for goodness' sake! I've been accused of wrongdoing in my life, and sometimes for good reason, but murder has never been one of my sins." She peered down at Samuel. "Where did you get such an idea?"

"You won't let me see the cellar." He didn't think it right to mention Joseph or the story of the murderous housekeeper. "And I know why you won't because that's where Mother is . . . that's where you put her after you killed her."

Samuel was crying now, his face buckled in grief, and he wanted nothing more than to dissolve into the bed. So he did the next best thing, pulling the covers over his face again.

"Enough." Ruth pulled the blanket down. "Who has put these ideas into your head? Who's making you think such nonsense?"

Samuel didn't answer.

"Is it that fool of a boy Joseph Collins?"

"No. I can think for myself."

"Well, if that's so, your thinking is leading you astray."

"Mother wouldn't stay away for all this time, not if she could help it. Something's happened to her, I know it has. She wants to be here, she wants to be with me, but she can't because she's rotting in the cellar."

"If I didn't know better, I'd say you'd been at the demon drink." Ruth shifted on the bed and put her arms on either side of Samuel. "I have not killed your mother and I haven't put her down in the cellar. She's in America and very much alive, just like I've been telling you. Haven't you been getting those lovely cards?"

"Yes."

"And didn't your mother tell you about the bankers in America that she hoped might be able to help with the factory?"

"Yes."

Ruth nodded. "Well, then?"

"She's been gone too long." He wiped his eyes as if that would stop the tears. "She didn't even say goodbye."

"Like I've told you too many times to count, it was all last-minute and your mother had to get to London by morning to catch the boat. If she had any idea how much it has upset you, I'm sure she'd feel wretched." Ruth sighed. "You miss her very much, I know that. You don't think I miss her, too? Every day I wish she were here, believe me, Samuel. She's like a force of nature, your mother, whizzing about the house turning everything upside down. I know I'm a poor substitute for a real mother, or a father, God rest his soul. But I'm doing the best I can, Samuel, and I don't pretend to be perfect . . . Sometimes things get said and done that we wish hadn't been said or done. But as I say, I'm doing the best I can. Do you understand?"

Samuel didn't offer a reply.

"I can't say how much longer your mother will be gone but I have a feeling you'll be hearing word from her very soon."

"I hope so," said the boy.

"Now let that be an end to it." Ruth stood up and tightened the cord of her dressing gown. "Friends?"

The boy felt there was little choice but to nod.

"Good. Now off to sleep."

She switched off the lamp, and in the half-light of the room, Samuel watched her silhouette move toward the door as if she were floating. She seemed to slow at the door, appearing to look back at him, but in the next breath, hardly the blink of an eye, was gone.

14

Samuel looked down at his plate, scrambled eggs and two sausages, wondering if a murderer could have made his favorite breakfast? Wasn't that a kind thing to do and very unlike a killer? But then he thought that in the whole history of the world, there must have been plenty of fine cooks who had murdered people and hidden their bodies.

"You've hardly touched your eggs." Ruth plunged the mop into the bucket and swished it about. "Aren't you hungry?"

"I am." He wasn't. Samuel was sitting at the kitchen table, in his usual place, but his eyes kept shifting across to the larder.

"I suggest you get on with it, then," said Ruth from behind him. "Your breakfast isn't going to fly up into your mouth unaided and you've still got to wash your face, comb your hair and change into your school uniform. All in the next twenty minutes."

"Yes, Ruth." Samuel made himself take another bite of food but it tasted like sand. How could he eat breakfast like nothing was the matter, when everything was?

"Don't forget to fetch your clean socks from the laundry," Ruth said. "I shudder to think what you get up to at school—all three pairs are full of holes. I've stitched them up as best I can, though I'm the first to admit, sewing isn't one of my gifts." She chuckled, which only added to Samuel's suspicions. "Mind you, I'd need to be a surgeon to mend some of those holes."

She pushed the mop across the floor and Samuel watched as it slithered over the pale stone like a hundred eels all moving as one. Even this made him think of his mother—he pictured the water rising in the cellar, dirty and cold, and washing over her. She was in the yellow dress she loved so much with the ivy along the trim, floating in the gray water, her eyes closed, her face white as snow, her lips a charcoal red.

He didn't want to believe his mother was dead. He wanted to believe what Ruth had told him—how she missed his mother, too, and how murder was not one of her sins. She looked so sure and calm when she spoke and wasn't it true that Ruth was about the most sensible person Samuel knew? And would a sensible person murder her employer and then hide the body in the cellar? He didn't imagine so.

But Joseph had said that some people were utterly bonkers and no one knew why.

For much of the night Samuel couldn't sleep. He lay there, wanting to feel deep down in his belly that Ruth was innocent, wanting the knot that was twisted there, all tangled up in the many days and nights his mother had been away from him, to slacken and unspool. He wasn't sure what a person telling the truth looked like exactly, but he thought they might look just like Ruth, sitting on the edge of his bed telling him his mind was muddled. And there were the postcards to consider. They had come from America and the handwriting was definitely his mother's. Didn't that make more sense than Joseph's story?

But he couldn't get past the cellar. Why hadn't Ruth let him see it? She knew how upset he was and she knew what he feared. So why not just unlock the door and prove that his mother wasn't down there? If Ruth had just let him see, Samuel felt sure it would have blown the dark thoughts away like a snuffed candle.

"Samuel?" Ruth was standing over him, her hands crossed over each other, resting on top of the mop.

"Yes, Ruth?"

"Did you hear what I said about the socks?"

He nodded.

"Are you feeling sick?"

He shook his head.

"You've got dark circles under your eyes and you look worn out." Ruth returned the mop to the bucket. "Did you have trouble sleeping last night?"

"I have a headache, that's all."

"Shall I give you something?"

"It's not that bad."

Ruth felt his forehead with the back of her hand and then his cheeks. "You don't have a fever."

"I'm not sick," said Samuel, his eyes once again returning to the larder.

"Well, your breakfast has gone cold and you've hardly eaten a morsel." Ruth picked up the plate and carried it to the sink.

Samuel stood. "I'll get ready for school."

"Yes . . . good."

The boy was almost at the door when Ruth called him back. She looked at him, her fingers touching the clover pin on her collar. "I know we settled things last night, about the cellar and all that nonsense concerning your mother. We did settle it, didn't we?"

It wasn't settled. Not one little bit. "Yes, Ruth."

"That's what I thought." Ruth licked her lips. "But I was thinking, it might set your mind at ease, now that you've calmed down and are thinking clearly, if we went down there and had a look. What do you think?"

It was as if Ruth had reached into his mind. "Can we go now?"

"I don't see why not."

The key caught in the lock and wouldn't budge. "Always gets stuck," Ruth muttered. Samuel stood behind her—the larder was too narrow for him to stand anywhere else—and waited for the door to open, his chest tingling, the nerves swelling his eyes until they stung for want of blinking.

With all the color drained from her fingers and her teeth pressed together, Ruth twisted the key as hard as she could. The lock released a piercing screech and yielded. "Thank heavens for that." Ruth glanced back at Samuel. "It's been so long since I was down here, the lock's awful rusted."

"Don't you come down when you need potatoes?" Samuel asked.

"Not always," Ruth said. "Usually I keep what I need up here in the larder. What I meant was, the lock is stiff because it's used so little. I'll have William see to it."

Ruth turned the handle and the narrow door swung open, leaving a black void in its place. "Pass me that flashlight, Samuel, before we both break our necks."

Samuel grabbed his father's flashlight off the shelf and passed it to Ruth. She turned it on, the pale beam practically swallowed up by the darkness. "Don't you come down until I turn the light on."

"I won't fall."

"Of course you won't. Whoever heard of anyone falling down a set of stairs in the pitch-dark?" She huffed as if the answer was perfectly obvious. "Wait until I turn the light on."

Wait? It took all of Samuel's self-control not to push Ruth aside and run ahead of her that very second. As for waiting in the larder, that was impossible. Stepping over the small wooden rise, Ruth lowered her head and stepped in, her eyes trained on the wooden stairs that tracked down into the gloom.

"Careful does it," she whispered.

Ruth began her descent and the boy followed quickly after her. She didn't make a fuss about it, probably too busy watching her step. The stairs had no railing and so they both needed the wall to steady themselves.

The rough wooden treads were worn smooth but they still murmured and creaked as Samuel and Ruth went down. An odor of damp and mold and the slow decay of things shut up in a windowless pit rose to meet them.

"Watch yourself, Samuel." Ruth had reached the bottom. "The last step catches you by surprise."

Just as the boy stepped onto the cellar floor, Ruth located a length of cord hanging from the ceiling. A single, unadorned light bulb bloomed into life. Samuel stood somewhere in the middle of the room and turned, taking in every detail. The room was about half the size of the kitchen, stone walls dripping with moss, a bare floor, a low ceiling that Ruth could have reached up and touched.

"Well?" Ruth was looking at the boy like he was about the silliest creature she ever saw. "Do you see a body? A bloody ax? Any chopped-up limbs?"

The cellar was littered with wooden crates and cardboard boxes and an open shelf with just a few bottles of dusty wine. Samuel walked around the room, opening crates, lifting the lids of boxes and moving a pile of old potato sacks from a dim corner. He found unused pots and pans, parts of lanterns, a broken side table, a few clocks, coarse sheets covered in a rainbow of splatter and the paint tins and stiff brushes that had caused them. What he didn't find, what wasn't there at all, was his mother. And this fact left him with a kind of emptiness that buffeted his body like a cold wind. He was happy and thankful, of course he was, but that emptiness meant that these things had nowhere to set down.

Ruth let the flashlight slacken in her hand. "As I told you last night, there is nothing here that would be of any interest to you."

That was true, Samuel had to admit, but there was something else, too. The cellar was just a smelly room full of discarded things, yet they were neatly organized. The crates against the wall, the boxes neatly clustered, even the floor was swept clean. Ruth would often say that the cellar was a mess she couldn't bear thinking about. But it wasn't a mess at all.

"Did you tidy up?" said Samuel.

The light from the bulb was rather harsh,

making the most of the thin lines around Ruth's eyes and mouth. "What?"

"It's tidy." Samuel looked about. "You said it was a great mess down here, but it's tidy."

Ruth sniffed. "You might consider this tidy, but I certainly don't."

Samuel had to admit that Ruth did have high standards when it came to what you might consider clean. "I just . . ."

"Samuel, look at me."

The boy did as he was told.

"Do you see any signs that there has been a corpse hidden down here?"

Samuel didn't offer a reply.

"Do I look like a crazed lunatic to you?"

That was very unfair because the boy had no experience with such things. Still, he couldn't deny that they were fair questions. He had wanted to see the cellar and now he had.

"Your mother is in Boston," said Ruth with calm certainty.

"I want her home."

"Yes, but you wishing it won't make it so. She's in Boston and she'll be there until things are sorted out with the steel mill." She saw the deep set of the boy's frown and it seemed to temper her resolve. "Of course, she might have completed her business and is sailing home this very moment."

Samuel bit on his bottom lip. "You really think so?"

"It's possible. I surely hope so." Ruth rubbed her brow. "Though I can't be certain, now can I? But I am sure about one thing—your mother is alive and well and one of these days she'll come gliding through the front door and prove it to you."

Ruth couldn't have said a more wonderful thing if she had tried and Samuel saw no reason not to smile. "I think so, too," he said.

Though the tugboat was barely an inch long it brimmed with authenticity. Like the much larger ship it belonged to, a replica of the RMS *Queen Mary*, the little boat was carved from wood in intricate detail and lovingly painted. The set belonged to Samuel's father and was given to Samuel on his seventh birthday on the understanding that it came with tremendous responsibility. As such, it was kept up on the mantel in his bedroom and almost never played with, no matter how it might call to him, practically crying out to be a part of some violent shipwreck that would require his whole battalion of fighter planes spiriting to the rescue.

The *Queen Mary* was still on the mantel, being much too big for what Samuel had in mind, but one of the four small tugboats that went with the set was nestled in the pocket of his school blazer. Samuel was still panting, having run all the way from his bedroom down to his mother's study.

He moved swiftly now, arranging the postcards around the atlas. With only a few minutes until he set off for school he had to be quick. And what he planned simply couldn't wait until the afternoon—not when this new certainty was swelling in his chest, demanding something solid that would carry him through the coming days as he waited for his mother to come home. And she was coming home. She was on the ship right that very moment, Ruth had practically guaranteed it.

Samuel picked up the coil of red yarn that he had taken from Ruth's sewing kit (there wasn't time to ask permission and there was no harm in it) and began pulling on the thread. The postcards were turned over and arranged in chronological order, though the boy didn't need to see the picture of each city to know the locations. Still, he checked, anyway, rattling off his mother's journey one destination at a time. With enormous care, Samuel began twisting the red yarn around the pin stuck in San Francisco. That was the first city his mother had visited. When it was secured to his satisfaction, he unspooled the yarn and pulled it toward Texas, winding it around the pin planted in the heart of Dallas. On and on he went, his nimble fingers working at speed, threading the red yarn across the atlas—back to California (this time Los Angeles), then on to Florida, Pennsylvania, Toronto, New York City, and only stopping once he had reached Boston.

The boy dug the tugboat out of his pocket. It wasn't exactly an ocean liner, not like the one his mother would be on, but it would do just as well. Samuel bit down on the yarn, severing it from the coil. Then he tied the end of the thread around the tugboat and placed in carefully on the atlas right over Boston Harbor. A grin pulled at his lips as Samuel pushed the boat out across the sea.

The little tugboat was bound for England and this thought shook the boy with a hope so fierce it made his eyes sting and flood with no thought for his dignity. But even this childish outburst was a blessing—for as a film of tears blurred Samuel's vision, he could just about see the blue of the page begin to ripple and churn, dissolving into a tide, the tugboat carving its way through majestic waters. It felt wrong to call it an atlas now, foolish, too, for it was really a world in miniature, and the story that it told was nothing short of wondrous. His mother was at sea, even as he was standing there in her study. He could see her out there on the ship's deck, clutching the railing and looking heartsick as she stared into the salty mist. She was saying his name over and over like the words of a treasured poem, laden with thoughts of her little man, and counting the days, minutes and hours until she was back home with him.

15

Samuel didn't walk straight home from school that afternoon. He spent more time than he needed packing his school bag and then sat down, tying and untying his shoelaces while the schoolyard emptied. If he stayed back an extra ten minutes or so, Joseph would get sick of waiting and would go on up the hill without him.

It wasn't that he didn't like Joseph; he was his best and only friend, after all. It was just that, without quite having the words to pin it down, Samuel knew he was carrying something terribly fragile and he feared that walking home with Joseph might break it. He wouldn't mean to do it or even know that he was doing it, but he would, because that was Joseph.

He waited as long as he could before passing out of the school gates, and when he did, Samuel collided with Mrs. Phillips and her basket full of groceries. Mrs. Phillips knew everyone in the village and she was one of the few people Samuel's mother would cross the street to avoid.

"You nearly knocked me over," she said, checking her bag to make sure her eggs hadn't broken (one had, which was nothing short of catastrophic). Then she looked him up and down. "I suppose your mother's not come back yet?"

"Not yet, Mrs. Phillips."

"What could possess her to sail halfway around the world on a whim?"

"Mother is meeting with—"

"She's had her troubles, we all know that." Mrs. Phillips said this more to herself than anyone else. "But what good is there in chasing rainbows? I told her that. Give up that wretched steel mill, that's what I said—it's beyond you. And do you know what your mother told me?"

Samuel didn't know.

"She said, 'How can I ever be happy stuck out here with barely two pounds to rub together? I'll go mad,' that's what she said. 'You'll find a way,' I told her. She said she had a plan to turn things around. A week later, I heard she went sailing to America without so much as a goodbye."

Samuel had never really liked Mrs. Phillips and he liked her even less now. She used a great many words and he wasn't sure any of them were good. "Mother will be home soon. Ruth says she's probably on the boat right now."

This caused Mrs. Phillips to smile rather coolly. "She would know, I suppose."

Luckily, Mrs. Phillips saw someone at the crossing she wanted to chastise even more than Samuel and he was able to escape. But though he was soon a safe distance from Mrs. Phillips, her words had their hooks into him and for some reason it made him think of his mother's letter.

The one he had hidden in the atlas. Why hadn't he taken it out and finished reading it? Didn't he go to a great deal of trouble and risk to steal it? In that moment, Samuel realized something he'd never known before—that it was possible to want to do something and not want to do it at the very same time.

"What's kept you?"

Samuel looked over and saw Joseph sitting in the shade of an elm tree. He shrugged. "I had things to do."

"What things?" Joseph got to his feet and picked up his bag.

"Just things."

Joseph fell in beside Samuel. "Mind if we don't run today? I'm dead tired. My dad was up to mischief last night."

"What sort of mischief?" Samuel asked.

"Drink mostly." Joseph nudged Samuel in the ribs. "You still spooked about old Ruth?"

"She's not old and I wasn't spooked."

"I don't blame you, not a bit. If my dad vanished into thin air and my mum said he'd gone off on a boat, I'd wonder if she'd done him in. Wouldn't blame her, neither."

Samuel couldn't let Joseph's words just hang there and mean what they meant, so he said the very things he didn't want to say. About Ruth catching him at the basement door and how he had accused her of being a murderer. Finally, he said, "Ruth showed me the basement this morning and there wasn't anything there."

He felt he had made perfect sense and that the matter was resolved. But then Joseph was looking at him with something like astonishment. "I can't believe she didn't kill you. But I suppose she couldn't do it right then and there. Where would she say you went?"

"Ruth didn't kill anyone, I just told you that." Samuel shook his head. "And I wouldn't have been snooping in that stinky cellar if it wasn't for you."

"I told you it was just a story, didn't I?"

"Ruth didn't kill anyone," Samuel said again.

"Never said she did. Thing is . . ." Joseph was the sort of boy who flew easily and willingly into intrigues, so it was impossible for him not to see the bloody potential in Samuel's story. "Thing is, Ruth didn't show you the cellar last night, did she?"

"It was very late," said Samuel.

They were at the steepest part of the hill now and both of them slowed, their breaths dissolving into faint puffs. "Even so, wouldn't it make sense to go down right then and there and get it over with? Isn't that what someone with nothing to hide would do?"

"Well . . ."

"Don't you see, Samuel, you gave old Ruth all night to clean out the cellar and get rid of your mum's—" Joseph stopped himself because there were some things even he couldn't say. "What I mean is, if there was anything down there she didn't want you to see, she could have gotten rid of it before sunrise."

Samuel was thinking of the cellar, swept clean, the boxes and crates neatly arranged. He didn't say any of this to Joseph.

"Of course, she would have needed help," said Joseph. "Getting rid of the evidence wouldn't be easy. Ruth's a solid sort but still, there's the stairs to think about and—"

"Shut up!" Samuel shouted this. "You talk a lot of rot, Joseph, that's what. My mother's in America and she's coming home any day now."

Despite the slope of the hill and the tightness in his legs, Samuel forced himself to walk faster, and in that way, Joseph quickly fell behind. Which was very satisfying.

"I was just saying, that's all!" Joseph sounded well out of breath. "You don't have to get so mad about it. I wouldn't be a friend if I didn't warn you when I smelled trouble."

The boy didn't look back. "There's no trouble."

"I hope you're right, that's for certain."

At the top of the hill, Samuel stopped and leaned against the gate to his house. He waited for Joseph, even though he was angry and had every right to be, because that's what friends do. They wait, even when they're mad. "See you tomorrow," mumbled Samuel.

"Meet you here at eight?" said Joseph, wiping the sweat from his neck.

Samuel nodded. He turned and began walking up the drive.

"Be careful, Samuel."

Samuel stopped, looking back. He thought he knew the answer but he asked it, anyway. "Careful of what?"

"I don't know exactly." Joseph had a faraway look that hinted at things unspoken. "Grown-ups can do rotten things sometimes." He shrugged. "Even the good ones, I reckon."

16

Ruth couldn't stomach lateness. It was one of the things guaranteed to get her hopping mad. She prided herself on being just where she said she was going to be at the very minute she promised. Turning up on time mattered and being late was as good as spitting in her eye. So when Samuel came up the drive, walking so slow you would think he had all the time in the world, when he was actually twenty minutes late, and she'd been worried half to death, it wasn't a great surprise that she would come marching out of the house with a grim look on her face. She'd been watching from the window, waiting on the boy so she could do just that.

"What time do you make it, Samuel Clay?" She was stalking across the lawn.

"I don't know," said Samuel, though he had a perfectly good watch on his wrist.

"It's ten past four. I've been worried sick, thinking you'd been run down or worse." She was looking the boy over, though Samuel couldn't think what she expected to find. "What's kept you? What were you doing all this time? I bet Joseph Collins had you up to no good."

The boy couldn't tell her that he had lingered in the schoolyard because then Ruth would ask why and no good could come of that. Luckily, he had another card to play. "Mrs. Phillips stopped me to talk."

This caused Ruth to roll her dark eyes. "That woman has no shame. I suppose she was full of questions about your mother?"

Samuel nodded.

"Well? What did she want to know?"

"When Mother was coming home."

Ruth sniffed. "And what business is it of hers?"

"Did you hear from Mother, Ruth? Did she write again?"

"There was nothing in the morning post." Ruth's scowl softened a little. "But I'm sure it won't be long now."

"Perhaps I should go to the post office and see if she has sent a telegram before she boarded the boat?"

"The boat? Samuel . . ." Ruth huffed. "If there was a telegram it would be delivered to the house. You know that very well as I've told you at least a dozen times this week alone."

"You promised I would hear from Mother soon. You said—"

"Don't start, Samuel. I'm in no mood." She glanced around and caught sight of William coming out of the woodshed with an ax. "Just be patient, your mother will . . . What on earth is that man doing?"

Ruth took off toward the woodshed, her arms

swinging the way they always did when she was on a mission. Samuel set his bag down and wandered after her.

"I hope you're not planning on wasting all afternoon chopping wood." Ruth was in the middle of saying this when Samuel reached her. "I wanted the lawn clipped today. If it gets much wilder, people will think the house has been abandoned."

"Hello there, Samuel." William pretended as if Ruth hadn't said a word.

William had been the gardener for as long as Samuel could remember. He was tall with bronzed hair that frequently looked in need of combing and a substantial beard. William was fond of squinting and he always seemed to be on the very edge of laughter. Samuel's father once said William could have made something of his life if he wasn't juggling quite so many vices.

"Hello, William," said the boy.

"Mr. Sloan, will you do as I asked?" Ruth's tone was crisp.

William smiled at her. "We can discuss it, once I've had a word with the boy."

Ruth and William didn't like one another. Last summer, Samuel had seen them in the stables having words. Ruth was angry, standing close to William—talking in a whisper, Samuel figured, which she always did when she was really cross. But William didn't seem scared at all. In fact, his hands were on her like she had taken something of his and he meant to get it back. Samuel had run and told his mother what he had seen, that Ruth might need help, but his mother had giggled and said Ruth was just fine and he had no business spying on people.

"How's life treating you, Samuel?" said William.

He always asked this question and Samuel usually shrugged, never sure how to answer it.

"I caught that rabbit of yours making a meal of my lavender this morning." William's grin suggested he wasn't especially bothered. "I had to turn the hose on him."

This made Samuel giggle.

Ruth huffed. "I lost a row of sprouts to that creature and it's not as if we have food to spare."

"Any more of them postcards from your ma?" William asked the boy.

Samuel nodded. "One came on Monday."

"How's she keeping over there in America?"

"She hates it. She wants to come home."

"I don't doubt it." For once, William didn't look amused.

"She'll be home soon," said Samuel. "Ruth says—"

"Mr. Sloan," said Ruth, her hands locked together, "I thought I made myself very clear about the lawn. Was I not clear?"

"My name's William." He swung the ax up onto his shoulder and looked at Ruth, a smile curling up under his mustache. "I seem to recall it's passed your lips once or twice."

Samuel saw the irritation splash over Ruth's face, her eyes narrowed, her cheeks flushed. "Mr. Sloan, are you not capable of trimming the lawn? Because if you're not, then I will."

"I doubt very much you'll find another gardener," William said. "They tend to like being paid and we both know I'm owed two weeks as of yesterday."

This seemed to take the wind out of Ruth's mighty sails. "As you know, Mr. Sloan, things have been rather difficult lately."

"I know it," said William, "and I've been patient, haven't I?"

Samuel watched the ax head turning back and forth as William twisted the handle.

"You have." Ruth cleared her throat. "I've let Olive go but it's all I can do to look after the boy and cook the meals and keep the house clean and tidy, without having to tend the garden, as well." She took a long breath. "That is why I need your assistance."

"Fair enough," said William. "But a man has to eat, Ruth, even a good-for-nothing like me. I can't be coming here, laboring from dawn 'til dusk, without payment."

Ruth glanced briefly at Samuel, then back at William. "I am working on it, Mr. Sloan."

"I've heard that before." William was smiling

121

again. "But if anyone can find a way, I reckon you can, *Miss* Tupper."

Ruth cleared her throat again and Samuel saw how uncomfortable she looked. He had an odd feeling then, one he couldn't put a name to. A sense that there was something passing between Ruth and William that wasn't about trimming lawns and paying wages, but something else. Something more.

"Will you get to work on the lawn like I asked?" said Ruth.

William nodded. "There's a dead branch on the elm by the gate and I reckon it'll fall if I don't see to it. I'll make a start on the lawn as soon as I'm done."

"Good." Ruth unclasped her hands. "Come along, Samuel, you have homework to do."

As Samuel wrote out his spelling words, his attention was elsewhere. He hadn't even touched the glass of milk or the shortbread in front of him. He was thinking about William and Ruth, wondering about what went unsaid between them, and those thoughts were like a net scooping up other ones and soon his mind was spinning darkly. Joseph was to blame. He'd said something as they walked up the hill. Something Samuel had thought was stupid but now had fixed itself to Ruth and William.

She would have needed help. Joseph was

talking about Ruth killing his mother and moving her body while Samuel was sleeping. Ruth would have needed help getting the body up the stairs. That was Joseph's theory. Samuel hadn't thought about that before. He'd just assumed Ruth was strong enough to do all the beastly work herself. She could lug sacks of flour from the car easily enough and carry in huge bundles of logs from the woodshed. When Joseph said what he did, Samuel had dismissed it as fanciful. Ruth hadn't done anything to his mother, and besides, who in the world would help her do such a horrid thing?

Then Samuel had watched Ruth and William giving each other strange looks, and Ruth blushing, William smiling at her and twisting the ax, and it all made horrible sense. Ruth had killed his mother and William had helped her hide the evidence. But where?

"It's not like you to leave a shortbread uneaten." Ruth was wiping down the kitchen table.

"I'm not very hungry," said Samuel.

"That's a first."

Samuel didn't want to believe it. Hadn't he stayed back from school just so Joseph wouldn't put doubts in his mind? If it felt odd for Samuel to have his mind changed so easily, his mother both alive and then dead from one breath to the next, he didn't question it. He had a great many thoughts and, in the course of any one hour, might feel ten different ways about the very same thing.

"I've finished my homework." Samuel closed his book. "Can I go outside and ride my bike?"

Ruth stopped cleaning the table and looked at him. "You've got no appetite for shortbread, but you've energy enough to ride your bike?"

Samuel picked a shortbread up and took a bite. "Can I go?"

"Suit yourself." Ruth rinsed the cloth out under the tap. "But make sure you change out of that school uniform first and don't throw your trousers on the floor. I want them folded and put away."

"Yes, Ruth."

The bike was leaning against the oak tree and Samuel walked right past it. He was looking for a body. He had already checked the stables but all he found were some engine parts, his father's car (which Ruth used to run messages in Penzance) and a wall of old cupboards filled with tools and jars of screws and nails.

That only left the woodshed and wasn't that the most likely place of all? No one went in there except for William and Ruth. The windows were painted over and it had a lock on the door. If Ruth needed to urgently move a body from the cellar, the woodshed was the perfect place to hide her wicked crime. So that was where Samuel was headed.

"Where are you going in such a hurry?"

William was across the yard, cutting the lawn just like Ruth had asked. He had worked up a sweat and was wiping his face with a dirty handkerchief.

Samuel stopped. "I'm looking for my bike."

"In the woodshed?"

Samuel didn't know what to say.

"I think I saw it by the oak tree." William wore a wry smile. "You must have walked right past it, I'd reckon."

"Oh." Samuel pushed the hair from his eyes. "I didn't see it."

"Daydreaming, were ya?"

Samuel nodded and then turned, walking back the way he had come. When he reached the oak tree, he walked around it and then, using the trunk as cover, snuck a peek at William. He was back at work on the lawn, heading down toward the fence. It was the perfect moment to go. Samuel sprinted across the grass, his shoes vanishing among the clusters of overgrown grass and wildflowers, his eyes fixed on the woodshed.

Samuel saw William turning the lawn mower— he'd have a clear view of him as soon as he looked up—so Samuel practically dove behind the woodshed, his knees skidding across the grass. He got up, caught his breath. Then he edged around the small stone building, his eyes fixed on the gardener. William wasn't looking over, his attention consumed by the task at hand, the roar of the mower as it sliced the tall grass causing the air itself to tremble. Samuel dropped low and crawled to the door.

He said a silent prayer to his father that it would be unlocked. Then another to his mother promising that he would find her and make Ruth and William, who were foul people with black hearts, pay for what they had done to her. His father must have been listening because the door opened easily.

The smell of freshly cut wood rushed at him when he stepped inside. It was a small room with bare walls and two windows painted green. Spiderwebs clung to the rafters and blurred the corners of the ceiling. Samuel lifted an old carpet rolled up by the door and moved the logs as best he could, checking every little place. He bent down, shifting a can of oil, and then inspected a sack slumped under the window. He didn't notice the hum of the lawn mower ceasing.

A hand gripped his shoulder, rendering him a block of stone.

"I guess it's not a bike you're looking for, then?" William was behind him.

Samuel forced himself to straighten up and turn around. "No."

That was the best he could manage.

William still had that faint smile on his face, his eyes shifting about the little room. "What are you up to, then?"

"I . . . I was fetching some wood for Ruth."

Samuel tried to look sincere. "She asked me to."

"Did she?" William scratched at his whiskers. "I cut a whole lot for her just last week and left it outside the kitchen door. Do you mean to say she's burned through it already?"

Samuel looked anywhere but at William.

"Seems to me you're in here for other reasons."

"I was playing."

William chuckled. "I've never known you to darken the door of my woodshed. What's the game, Samuel?"

"Well . . ." Samuel's mind whirled until it found what he was looking for. "I was pretending that there's buried treasure somewhere in the garden and I have to find it before sundown or it will disappear." He swallowed hard, which didn't help. "It's magic treasure, you see."

"Magic, you say?"

Samuel nodded.

"Ah." William looked around the woodshed again and then his calloused hand ruffled the boy's hair. "I'll let you get on with it, then."

William went to leave, then turned back. "Forgot why I came in here in the first place." Holding the doorframe, he bent and picked up the can of oil. "The blades are sticking."

Samuel watched William walk across the lawn. He had almost reached the lawn mower when he looked around and shouted, "But if you find any of that treasure, I want half. Deal?"

Samuel nodded from the doorway.

"Good lad."

Samuel resumed his search, checking the cupboard where William kept his axes and then looking everywhere else again and then one more time. His heart still thumped wildly—William catching him was responsible for that—and a great quickening coursed about his body, making it hard to keep still. But among the great jumble of feelings stirring at the heart of this storm was but a single thought. His mother wasn't there.

17

Samuel crossed the hall and began to climb the stairs, his steps slow and lumbering, on account of his folly. How stupid he'd been to think that Ruth and William were up to no good. He'd moved the bike from under the oak tree so that it would look like he had really been riding it. Ruth noticed things like that. As he walked, he made a promise to himself. It was time to stop thinking that Ruth was a monster. She wasn't lying to him, she hadn't hurt his mother—she was just Ruth, same as always.

At the top of the stairs, Samuel turned right on the landing and headed down the corridor toward his bedroom. Perhaps he would ask Ruth for another shortbread now that his appetite had returned. But first, he wanted to play with his planes for a while, not worrying about anything at all. And he would have done just that, if not for the light slipping across the floor. It was coming from an open door, bright sunlight spilling out and up the wall. Only it wasn't Samuel's bedroom door that was open. Nor was it Ruth's. It was his mother's.

Samuel slowed down as he got close, going up on his tiptoes without really thinking about it. The door was half-open; a key was fixed in the lock and there were noises coming from inside. Samuel put a hand to his mouth to halt the squeal from coming out. His mother. She had come home and was unpacking that very moment, probably tired from her long voyage and wanting to freshen up first before she came to find him.

There was no need to tread carefully, not now. Samuel pushed on the door and walked in. But he must have been quieter than he intended because she did not hear him. She was across the room at the chest of drawers. Her back was to Samuel and she was pulling open the top drawer, peering down with great interest, her hands vanishing inside.

"What are you doing?" Samuel asked.

Ruth's head flew up and she gasped, spinning around. Samuel had never seen her look so pale. "Samuel." She was clutching her chest. "You scared the life out of me."

"What are you doing?" he asked again.

"Well . . ." Ruth glanced at the open drawer. "It's my clover pin, you know the one?"

Samuel nodded.

"It's gone, don't ask me how, and I'm desperate to find it. I've looked all over, turned the house upside down, I have, but it's nowhere to be found."

Ruth's pin wasn't on her collar. Samuel knew it was a gift from her father and she wasn't ever without it, so it made sense that she would "turn the house upside down" to get it back. But there was a problem.

"Why would you think your pin was in Mother's drawer?" Samuel wandered over to the marble fireplace, touching the cold mantel.

"Why do you think, Samuel?" Ruth pushed the drawer closed. "As you know, I caught you snooping in here just the other day and it was me who returned those letters to this very drawer. Can you blame me for thinking the pin might have fallen in?"

"That was two days ago. You had the pin on yesterday—I saw it."

"Well, maybe I did." Ruth patted down her hair. "I've been so sick with worry I'm not thinking straight. That pin means the world to me and, as I said, I've looked everywhere else."

"Perhaps it's in the cellar. Did you look there?"

"What? Don't talk nonsense, Samuel." Ruth crossed the room, throwing the boy a fierce look as she passed him. "It was my grandmother's pin, given to me by my father just before he passed, and if I don't find it, I'll never forgive myself."

"I thought Mother had come home." Samuel's eyes were fixed on the chest of drawers.

"Well, you were wrong." Ruth's sigh was full of provocation. "Come along, I have to get dinner started."

Samuel made his way to the door. "Don't you want to keep searching for your pin?"

"I haven't time." Her voice was harsh now.

She pressed herself against the door and let Samuel pass out into the corridor. Then she pulled it shut, locked it and placed the key in the pocket of her apron.

"I thought you were her." Samuel's eyes roamed the housekeeper's face. "When I walked in, I thought you were Mother standing there."

"Wash up and tidy your room before dinner. Is that clear?"

Ruth walked quickly down the corridor, her shoes tapping the floor like the ticks of a racing clock. Samuel thought he heard her muttering to herself but he couldn't be sure. She turned at the landing, her head bent low, disappearing down the stairs. The boy stood there long after she had gone, thinking on it all, and watching the shadows gather in the empty spaces where she had been.

18

Steam rose up off the lamb's scored flesh, the blistered skin largely hidden beneath sprigs of rosemary. "Hungry?"

Samuel was thinking about his mother again. Catching Ruth going through that drawer had cracked open everything he had fixed back together. Was she after his mother's letters? Was there something in them that she wanted to find? Or to hide? Ruth said she was looking for her pin, that it might have fallen in there when she put the letters back, but Ruth had that pin yesterday and she wore it every day. So she couldn't have lost it in his mother's bedroom two days ago.

"Samuel, I asked if you were hungry."

"Yes." Then he said, "Not really."

This caused Ruth to look down at him and scowl. "But you love my lamb roast."

Samuel nodded and had the good sense to say, "It looks delicious."

"Well, then, I suggest you rediscover your appetite because it's the last piece of good meat we're likely to get for some time. Mr. Oldfield has closed our account at the butcher." She huffed. "Waving the bill about in front of half the village like I was a common criminal." Her nostrils flared and her lips faded to a faint line.

"He won't let me buy so much as a rabbit until the account is paid in full. Hateful man."

The boy's mind was too crowded to make room for a butcher, even a hateful one. When he had surprised Ruth, she had jumped, and when she turned around she looked pale and scared. Ruth never looked scared. Samuel had caught her doing something she wasn't supposed to, and that could only mean one thing.

"Did you tidy your room like I asked?"

He hadn't. "Yes, Ruth."

"You haven't touched that Bible in two days. Reverend Pryce will be at school on Monday and you know he's awarding a prize for the best writing and another for the best drawing. When are you planning on finishing it?"

"Soon."

"Tomorrow before school and no complaints." Ruth picked up a large carving knife from the table. "One piece or two?"

Samuel asked for two, knowing it would please her. He watched as she pushed the fork into the lamb, the animal's pale blood rushing up around it, and then sliced through the meat, the flesh parting with ease.

Grown-ups can do rotten things sometimes. That's what Joseph had told him. *Even the good ones.* Samuel didn't understand everything, but he was sure bad things were happening around him. His mother had been gone much too long. When she had told him that his father was dead, hadn't she said that it was just the two of them now? That they only had each other, and when two people have just each other, why would one of them sail across the world without so much as a goodbye?

"I have gravy on the stove." Ruth pointed with the tip of the knife. "Fetch it for me."

"Yes, Ruth."

Samuel got up and walked over to the stove, picking up the pot. Ruth said that his mother was in America but he didn't believe that was true. Not anymore.

"Mind you don't burn your hand on that," Ruth said.

"It's not that hot."

Ruth sniffed and let the knife go limp in her hand. "I thought we might go to the park and feed the ducks on Saturday, once I'm finished at the market. Would you like that?"

Samuel nodded.

She was giving him a look now. "You're not out of sorts about that business upstairs, I hope?"

"No."

"From the frown on your face, it's clear that something's got you in a mood." Ruth pierced a slice of lamb and laid it on Samuel's plate. The sound of the knife sliding down the fork to release the meat sparked a shiver that raced right through the boy. "You'd think it was you who'd lost a precious family pin and not me."

"Perhaps it's in your bedroom," said Samuel, sitting down. "I could help you look for it."

"You think I haven't looked there myself? I've turned the whole room upside down."

"Maybe it's not lost at all."

Ruth glared at him. "What's that supposed to mean?"

"Mother says that just because you can't find a thing doesn't mean it's lost."

Samuel watched the knife moving about in Ruth's hands. "Sounds like nonsense to me."

He wanted to tell her that he wasn't going to let her keep pretending this was her house for very much longer. He didn't, though, because he could see the nasty glint in Ruth's eye and, even lost in the wilderness of his troubles, he knew when to shut up. Besides, he had a plan now. All he needed was help.

19

"Felix Clay."

"Do you have the number?"

"No. His name is Felix Clay," whispered Samuel. "From Penzance."

The operator let out a faint moan. "Hold on."

Samuel took the telephone from his ear and listened. Down past the stairs he could hear Ruth moving about in the kitchen, plates clanging together, taps running, still cleaning up after dinner. Samuel had rushed through the meal and quickly excused himself. That hadn't gone unnoticed.

"You don't want a mince pie?" Ruth asked.

Samuel shook his head. "Not tonight. Shall I go and get ready for bed?"

"I've never heard that before." Ruth picked up his plate. "Off you go, then."

There hadn't been a great deal of talk during the meal. Ruth didn't seem in the mood and Samuel was trying his best not to look like he was up to mischief. Every now and then Ruth's hand would go up to her collar as if she expected her pin to be there, and when it wasn't, she would take her hand away quickly as if she was foolish to have forgotten.

"I'm connecting you now," said the operator.

She was gone before Samuel could say thank you, replaced by a loud crackle, then silence, then the pulsing sound of a ringing phone. Samuel stole another look down the hall.

"Hello," came a voice.

"Uncle Felix?"

"Sammy?"

"Yes."

"Well, this is a surprise. How are you, ducky?"

"I think something's happened to Mother."

"What's that, Sammy? Sorry, I've got some people over. Just a little get-together before I head off to London."

"Samuel?" It was Ruth. "Samuel?"

Samuel heard her footsteps on the stone floor.

"Sammy, are you there?" said Uncle Felix down the telephone.

The hall was in darkness, barely a sliver of moonlight rippling about the vast chamber. Samuel pressed himself against the wall.

"Samuel?" Ruth had her head poked out of the kitchen door and was peering into the darkness. "Samuel, is that you?"

The boy didn't move, didn't say a word.

"Sammy?" Uncle Felix seemed to be talking to people at his end; there was a hum of voices, but Samuel didn't catch the words. Then he said, "I think he's gone."

Ruth kept peering into the shadows, the light from the kitchen catching her thin lips, and

Samuel was certain she was about to walk into the hall for a closer look—she had no tolerance for unexplained noises. But then she huffed and vanished from the doorway.

"I'm still here," whispered Samuel.

"Thought I'd lost you there, Sammy." His uncle chuckled. "Are you in church, ducky? I can hardly hear you."

Samuel heard muffled laughter in the background.

"I think something has happened to Mother," Samuel said.

"Why? Have you heard something?"

"No, but I think that Ruth—"

"Has Ruth heard something?"

"No, that's not what I—"

"Would you like me to have a word with Ruth? Is that it? Put her on, there's a good chap."

"No, I can't do that."

Samuel wanted to tell his uncle about the housekeeper in Germany and how his mother had gone without saying goodbye and Ruth was the only one to see her go and how he had caught her in his mother's bedroom. But the words never did come out right. Not when he needed them.

"Uncle Felix, where's my mother?" The boy's voice was barely a whisper. "Do you know? Can you tell me, please?"

"Where is she? In America, I should think. Unless she's gone somewhere else looking for her pot of gold."

"I don't think so," said the boy softly.

"Listen, ducky, things are rather noisy at my end. Why don't I call you when I get back from London and we'll have a good chat then?"

"She's been away one hundred and eighteen days, Uncle Felix. She wouldn't stay away so long if she could help it."

"Well, that's business for you, isn't it?" Uncle Felix chuckled again. "Don't understand it myself, but you mustn't lose heart, Sammy. I'm sure your mother will be home in a jiffy. Now I must dash."

"Please, listen—something has happened, I know it has."

The was a loud crackle down the line. ". . . talk when I get back from London the week after next. That's a promise, Sammy. Get some sleep, won't you? You sound worn out."

The phone clicked and the line went dead.

20

Sleep wouldn't come and Samuel lay in bed for an eternity looking up at the ceiling. Even the shadows from the oak tree outside, reaching across the ceiling like the talons of some malevolent sorceress, weren't fearsome enough for him to shut his eyes. How could he sleep? It was foolishness to even try. His mind was a tempest of wild contemplation.

When Ruth came up to check on him, he pretended to be asleep. Which was a waste of time.

"You don't fool me, Samuel Clay," she said. "I know when you're asleep and I know when you're trying to make it look like you are."

He opened his eyes. Ruth was standing over his bed, holding a cup and saucer, and Samuel knew it contained tea with the juice of a full lemon squeezed into it. Ruth took one with her to bed every night.

"Did you brush your teeth?" she asked.

Samuel had nodded.

"I see you were telling tales about tidying your room." She was scowling at the planes scattered across the floor in battle formations and soldiers lying facedown. "No good can come from lying, Samuel, haven't I told you that a thousand times?"

"Don't you ever lie?" It seemed a fair question.

Ruth scooped up two or three of the planes with her free hand, placing them on the side table. "Not if I can help it."

But that wasn't really an answer and Samuel knew it. Perhaps the doubt played on his face because Ruth added, "Of course, there are times when it isn't right to speak the full truth. To protect someone's feelings and such."

"Protect them from what?"

"Well," said Ruth, taking a sip of her tea, "sometimes the very worst thing you can tell a person is the truth, especially if it will do more harm than good. My sister Alice once asked me what I thought of the dress she was wearing to a special dance. Now, the dress was nice enough but her hair was frightful and her makeup brought to mind a carnival clown—and I said so." Ruth sniffed. "That went down like a lead balloon."

"She was angry?"

"Oh, yes. I realized too late that some people, like my sister Alice, aren't ready for the truth. Which is what I was trying to tell you." She straightened her shoulders. "Mind you, I still prefer to speak my mind and suffer the consequences."

The boy was staring up at her. "Have you ever lied to me?"

"What a thing to ask!"

"Have you?"

Ruth rested the cup on the saucer. "Never. Now it's time you were asleep."

It might have been time but there was no sleeping for Samuel. Each worry heaped atop the next, until it felt like there was a great mass pushing down on him, stealing the breath from his lungs.

He thought about his mother's letter. Buried within the ornate curves of her words he sensed an undeniable jeopardy, though he couldn't name what exactly. But Ruth had been riffling through his mother's drawer, which meant she must have been looking for that letter. Perhaps it contained something she didn't want Samuel to discover. Some clue about what Ruth had done to his mother. Or where she really was.

The boy stood up and another notion quickly hurried in, as they tended to do—Ruth didn't know that Samuel had stolen the letter, because if she did, he would surely have heard about it by now and felt her wrath. Which meant that Ruth didn't know about the letter; so perhaps that wasn't what she was after. Still, Samuel felt that there was now nothing more urgent in the world than reading what his mother had written to his father. And that's what he intended to do.

The door to his bedroom squeaked with treacherous glee as Samuel stepped into the corridor. The floorboards, too, seemed determined to betray him, creaking and moaning as if he were crawling along an aching back.

Samuel passed his mother's bedroom first, a dark tomb. And for some reason this was a relief. As if a part of him instinctively knew he could not carry the burden of another fresh mystery that night. But Ruth's bedroom had a story to tell. A faint blush of lamplight bloomed beneath her door.

He didn't intend to stop. There was nothing unusual about Ruth being up late. Quite often, when Samuel had gotten up to use the toilet, he would see Ruth's light on. So why did it seem to call to him now? He didn't know. Samuel crept toward the door. Then he shut one eye, while the other found the keyhole.

It was an oval-shaped view, the orb blurring the edges of the bedroom. He saw the bed, still made, and the window across the room and the table under it. And he saw Ruth sitting there, in her nightdress, her hair out. A lamp was switched on and a dark bottle perched beside her—it looked just like the expensive wine his parents would drink at dinner. The same wine his mother said made his father prone to unsettling fits of national pride and falling asleep midsentence. Ruth was looking down, her usually straight shoulders hunched over, her right elbow bent and moving. Samuel supposed she was writing.

It wasn't so very odd to be writing a letter at

night, he reasoned. People did it all the time, didn't they? Perhaps Ruth was writing to her sister Alice, who was getting married soon and for the second time (which wasn't a scandal because her first husband had fallen under a train). So why did watching Ruth, fully occupied with the writing of something, twist the knot in his stomach? It wasn't fear—what was there to be afraid of?—it was something far more urgent. Samuel needed to know what she was writing because he couldn't imagine a world in which this late-night labor didn't have something to do with his mother.

His hand gripped the doorknob. He knew she would be furious if he barged in; she might beat him, throw him across the room. She'd done that before. He wanted not to care; he wanted to be brave and take what she might give him, if it meant knowing what she was up to. But just as the tide had carried him to Ruth's door and practically pushed him up to the keyhole, it drifted out just as suddenly. Now, barging into Ruth's bedroom felt like a reckless idea. The hour was late and he could get his mother's letter and take it to his room and that would be enough, at least for tonight. That's what he told himself.

Samuel took his hand off the doorknob. But just like the creak of his bedroom door and the snap of the floorboards, the handle had no regard for his wish to slip away unnoticed. It was loose—Ruth was always meaning to fix it—and so it rattled. Not loudly or a lot. But enough.

Through the keyhole Samuel saw Ruth's head lift. She opened the drawer in front of her, put away whatever she was writing and looked back at the door, her eyes narrowing darkly. It was as if she was looking right at him. But she couldn't see him through the keyhole, could she? When Ruth shot up, her chair flew back, scraping along the floor and tilting back against the bed. Samuel pulled away. He heard Ruth's rapid footsteps as she ran across the room, pounding like war drums. He was running, too, tearing down the hall. Ruth's door flew open, just as he lunged through his own door, shutting it.

His back was pressed to the door, his breathing hurried, his throat so dry that swallowing was an ordeal. Ruth would surely hear him if he tried to reach his bed. It was too late to do anything but keep utterly still and quiet. Outside, he listened for Ruth. She wasn't running now, and he guessed from the occasional crack of the floorboards that she was moving. But slowly.

"Who's there?" Ruth's voice was more a hiss than a whisper. "Samuel, is that you?"

Her footsteps drew closer. Samuel tried to steady his chest but every time he shut his mouth the breath would just about burst out of him. There was silence for a moment and the boy wondered if Ruth was still there. Then the boards groaned just outside his door. The door handle rattled and began to turn, its hideous screech snatching the strength from his legs. Samuel closed his eyes, held his breath.

A loud bang broke the silence.

He heard Ruth gasp. "Pa?" That's what she whispered. "Pa?"

Samuel couldn't say for sure, but he supposed the chair in her bedroom must have fallen over. The doorknob twisted back into place and then he heard rapid footsteps moving away from him. The surge of relief was so powerful it made him dizzy. He felt the door at his back, and though the danger had passed, he stayed frozen to the spot, the only movement the rapid rise and fall of his chest. It was a good minute or two before he dared to cross the room and crawl into bed.

He hadn't been lying there long when the door opened and Ruth came in. The boy was lying on his side and did his best to breathe slowly, deeply, and look fast asleep. He felt the lamplight slip over his face and he heard her own breathing, which was more rapid than his, and smelled the sourness of her breath. Ruth stayed there for some time—he didn't know how long—just looking at him. Then she muttered something—he thought he heard the word *nonsense*—and walked from the room, closing the door behind her.

Samuel kept his eyes shut long after she had left; he didn't dare move or make a sound. He just lay there pretending to be asleep, fully aware that this was a wise thing to do, as there was every chance Ruth was watching him through the keyhole.

21

Ruth was bright and cheerful at breakfast, which wasn't like her at all. She moved about the kitchen in good spirits, even making a low sound every now and then, like she was singing softly to herself.

"How did you sleep?" she asked Samuel when he sat down at the table.

"Okay."

"I'm all out of eggs. There's no butter left, either." Ruth put a plate down in front of Samuel with two sausages on it and some bread. "You didn't hear any loud noises?"

Samuel kept his eyes on the bread. "What kind of noises?"

"Oh, nothing." Ruth released a short laugh. "I was reading in bed and must have fallen asleep. The book slipped from my fingers and hit the floor with a mighty bang. Loud enough to wake the dead, it was." She took a seat at the table, the steam from her bowl of porridge rising up like a chimney pot. "It didn't wake you?"

"No."

"Good."

"I had a strange dream last night." He hadn't, of course, but it was as if Ruth's lie was a spark that ignited the boldest part of him. "At least, I think it was a dream . . . It felt real, though."

Ruth took a spoonful of porridge, then wiped her mouth with a napkin. "What was the dream about?"

"A ghost," said the boy softly.

"A ghost?" Ruth tilted her head.

"It was outside my bedroom door, walking up and down the hall."

"If the dream troubled you, then you'd best not dwell on it," said Ruth quickly.

"The ghost was white as snow, with long hair and breath so rotten it could knock you down. It was an angry ghost, Ruth, full of riddles that crawled along its flesh like maggots."

"That will do, Samuel. This sort of talk doesn't belong at a breakfast table."

"The ghost walked back and forth along the corridor, glowing like a lantern, and even though the ghost had no feet, I could hear its boots creaking on the wooden floor. I thought the ghost was coming to get me, you see, and I was scared . . . I heard it whispering something over and over."

"What a horrible dream." Ruth said this with such sharp certainty it could only mean the subject was closed. "You best eat those sausages before they go cold."

The boy looked only at Ruth. "Do you know what the ghost whispered in my dream, Ruth? Do you know what it said over and over?"

"Eat your breakfast, Samuel." Ruth was churning

the porridge with her spoon. "You've still got to get dressed for—"

"*Pa.*"

Ruth's eyes clouded over, her lips pressed tight.

"That's what the ghost said as it walked the halls. *Pa! Pa! Pa!*"

"Enough!"

Ruth threw the spoon down with such force porridge flew out, landing on the table. The might of her anger seemed to reach out and push Samuel back in his chair.

"I'll hear no more of your dreams, Samuel Clay." Ruth was gripping the edges of the table like she was trying to hold herself in place. "Something's haunting you, boy, but I doubt very much it's a ghost who's to blame."

The hair fell over Samuel's eyes and he did not push it away. "What is it, then?"

"You tell me and we'll both know."

"I want Mother."

"She isn't here!" Ruth shouted. "You are here and I am here, God help me, but your mother isn't and all your asking and wanting and fretting isn't going to bring her back before she's good and ready."

Every word was a dagger scoring his flesh. How cleverly Ruth could say a thing so it was true and cruel all at once. "I'll tell Mother. I'll tell her what—"

"She can't hear you, not where she is," said

Ruth coldly, "and I've had my fill of talking about her."

It was a cowardly thing to do, he knew that, but sometimes the cowardly thing was the only way to keep from going under. Samuel jumped up and ran from the kitchen.

"Is that all?"

The boys were sitting at the base of the hill, beneath the shade of the elm tree, trying to figure things out. Samuel had shared news of the night before and what he had seen and Joseph was bitterly disappointed.

"She heard a noise and went out to see if anyone was there." He was poking at the dirt with a stick. "It's not like she knocked down your door and came running in with blood all down her nightdress and a knife in her hand. Now, that would be something."

"She came to my door," said Samuel, tucking his legs up and hugging them. "She had her hand on the doorknob and everything. If it wasn't for that noise she would have come in."

"Still don't mean she was going to kill you."

"I heard her say *Pa*." Samuel hugged his legs tighter. "And when I told her about the dream I pretended to have, she got so angry. I was sure she was going to . . ."

"What?"

"I don't know. Something."

Samuel had confessed everything to Joseph on the walk to school. Well, all except for what Ruth said about his mother.

"Didn't you say old Ruth's father was dead?" said Joseph.

"Yes, I think he died when she was young."

"Well, don't you see? Ruth heard you rattle the doorknob and she thought it was the ghost of her dad come to visit her."

Joseph had a great many foolish ideas but this wasn't one of them.

"Some people want to be haunted," continued Joseph. "That's what my mum says."

He hadn't known he was doing it but Joseph's words brought the color to Samuel's cheeks. *Something's haunting you, boy.* Ruth had said that very thing.

"When I found her in Mother's bedroom," Samuel said, "she looked scared. Truly scared. I caught her doing something she didn't want me to see."

"She's a sneaky one, old Ruth." Joseph allowed a faint nod of admiration. " 'Course, she might really have been looking for her pin. Could be innocent enough."

"She lies, Joseph. Last night, Ruth said that she was reading in bed and that her book fell on the floor, but I know that wasn't true. She was writing at her desk . . . only I don't know what."

Joseph shrugged. "Grown-ups lie all the time.

Maybe she was writing in a diary, confessing all her secrets, that sort of thing. Everything she doesn't want anyone else to know." The furious potential of this idea caused the boy to sit up and hit the ground with the stick. "Did you see what she did with it?"

"With what?" Samuel's mind was elsewhere.

"The diary, stupid."

"Ruth put whatever it was in a drawer."

Joseph nudged Samuel in the arm. "If you could get hold of that diary, you'd know whether old Ruth was up to no good. I reckon if she murdered anyone, she'd be just the sort to put it all down on paper. You know, so she could read it back when she's old and remember all the rotten things she's done."

This notion had much to recommend it, being sinister and perfectly aligned to Samuel's own prejudices, so the boy could hardly stop himself from reaching out and grabbing hold.

22

When he got home from school, Samuel didn't ask if there had been word from his mother. He didn't dare after what happened at breakfast. Instead, he went straight upstairs to get changed and then went out into the yard looking for Robin Hood. The rabbit was resting under the hedge and it was some consolation to feed it a full leaf of cabbage and marvel at a creature so utterly free. Samuel only ventured back inside when his hunger was intolerable, overpowering his dread of seeing Ruth.

He found her spreading icing on a small chocolate cake. "Thought you'd smell this baking and be in here half an hour ago," she said.

Samuel walked silently into the kitchen. Yes, he very much wanted a slice of that cake, but seeing Ruth brought what happened hurrying back to him and the spark of outrage was soon aglow.

"How was school, then?" Ruth asked.

"Boring." Samuel sat down, his arms folded.

"I see." Ruth scattered a rainbow of sprinkles over the rich dark icing. She was wearing the thinnest of smiles. "You've nothing to learn, I suppose? You know all there is to know in the world?"

Samuel hadn't said that. He'd just said it was boring, which was entirely truthful.

"All done." Ruth wiped her hands on her apron and looked over at Samuel. "Would you like a slice?"

Of course he wanted a slice, but he couldn't bring himself to say so.

"Not hungry?" Ruth said.

"A bit," muttered Samuel.

"Thought so." Ruth's smile was smug and that made Samuel want to throw the cake right in her face. "Can you guess who I met in the village this morning?"

How was Samuel supposed to know such a thing? But then he thought it might have to do with his mother, news of some sort, and once that thought had shown up there was no other choice than to say, "Who?"

"Mrs. Collins." Ruth went to the cupboard, pulling out a plate. "We had a lovely chat outside the post office."

Something about the way Ruth was talking, the lightness in her voice and the breezy smile on her face, began to unsettle him. "What did you talk about?"

"Lots of things." Ruth put the plate on the table and got a knife from the drawer. "She told me that Joseph spends a great deal of time prattling on about you."

Samuel watched as Ruth cut a generous slice of chocolate cake and set it down on the plate. He said, "Oh."

"Oh, indeed." Ruth passed the cake to Samuel. "Mrs. Collins told me that her Joseph is convinced I've got dead bodies piled up in the cellar." She looked only at Samuel. "Can you imagine that?"

The boy stayed quiet.

"Joseph's mother thought the whole thing was hilarious and, naturally, I enjoyed the joke along with her." Ruth retrieved a fork from the drawer, handing it to Samuel. "Though it's hard to find the funny side of an ugly, wicked lie." She smiled. "Eat up, I know it's your favorite."

Although his appetite had left him, Samuel took a bite, occupying himself wholly with the cake and not watching Ruth as she moved about the kitchen.

"Can you think where your friend Joseph might get a story like that, Samuel?"

Samuel's mouth was mercifully full so it made not answering an easier matter.

Ruth was at the sink now, running the knife under the water. "Cat got your tongue? I asked you where Joseph got such an idea?"

"I don't know."

"You don't know?"

"Yes. I mean, no."

"Because I've been thinking about it all day and I came to the conclusion that perhaps someone from this house told Joseph that ridiculous story."

Which wasn't true at all. The story had come

157

from Joseph, but as Samuel didn't have the self-preserving instincts of a traitor, he refused to say so.

"Look at me, Samuel." Ruth's voice was hard as flint.

The cake was delicious but he was not enjoying it one little bit. Samuel lifted his head.

"It is bad enough that I have to hear the foolishness that comes out of your mouth night and day." She was pointing at him with the knife; water dripped from it onto the floor. "But I will not have you spreading this nonsense all over the village so that I have to suffer it there, as well. What do you suppose would happen if someone other than Mrs. Collins heard such a story?"

The boy didn't have an answer for that.

"They would call the police, who would come here and see that there's not an ounce of truth to the story and then . . . well, then they would want to see you and do you know why?"

Samuel shook his head.

"Because they would think you had an illness of the mind, Samuel. They would think you were a very sick boy, because a healthy mind wouldn't harbor such dark thoughts, and I fear you would be taken from this house and put in a hospital and you might never come back. Is that what you want?"

The room was suddenly a cold chamber and Samuel felt the bumps rising on his flesh. He didn't want to believe Ruth, but she sounded so sure, and so worried for him, and wouldn't she know such things? "I don't want that," he said.

"Don't you? Well, then, you better hope it goes no further than it already has." Ruth dropped the knife into the sink. "Though gossip is like a honey pot to a swarm of bees in this village." She was scowling now. "Have you told this awful story to anyone else?"

"No, Ruth."

"You swear it?"

"Yes, Ruth."

"That's something, I suppose." The tight lines around her mouth softened. "Let's say no more about it, then."

Samuel found himself nodding.

"Why don't you finish your cake, then get on with your homework." Ruth was busy at the sink and her indignation seemed to have stalled. "You'll note that it's chocolate—your favorite, no less."

This made Samuel think of the last chocolate cake Ruth had made—or tried to, anyway—and how it had shattered on the floor after she had grabbed his arm and thrust him against the table, and the rage on her face because she had told him to stop running and enough was enough. Samuel felt the tension in his belly and his hunger deserted him. Still, he knew that Ruth would like to see him eat the cake; she was watching and it was his favorite. So he picked up the fork and took another large bite.

"How is it?" she asked before he'd even had a chance to swallow.

"Good."

Ruth went to the larder and came out with a handful of onions. "I'm cooking pie with the leftover pork tonight—there's plenty left and I can throw in a few bits and pieces to liven it up."

Samuel watched Ruth as she went to the chopping block and began peeling the onions. She had her back to him but her head lifted every now and then as she spoke. "I had planned on roasting a pheasant with fresh greens but . . ." She sighed. "Pheasant costs more than I can spare right now, and there's the outstanding bill at Mr. Oldfield's to consider, so leftovers it is."

"Are we poor?" Samuel took another bite of cake.

"Things are tight. But we're not destitute. Not quite, at any rate."

The good cheer suddenly washing about the kitchen didn't do a great deal for Samuel's spirits. Everything Ruth had said about the police coming and locking him away in some revolting hospital had bruised and he had to force himself to take another bite of cake.

"Now, I don't want you saying anything about leftovers to Joseph Collins, either," instructed Ruth. "I'm sure the whole village has heard about my public shaming at the butcher's, so we don't want to add fuel to the fire. Is that clear, Samuel?"

Samuel swallowed the cake quickly so that he could answer Ruth and immediately he felt a strange sensation in his throat. Something odd, something foreign, had passed down and then got stuck. It lodged there and would not move, no matter how hard Samuel swallowed. He was so busy trying to force it down that he didn't notice how the air no longer moved freely. His face felt hot and now he was trying desperately to force a breath up from his lungs.

Ruth lifted her head but did not turn around. "I said, is that clear, Samuel?"

He was making a gurgling sound—at least, he was trying—but it quickly died without the breath to carry it.

"What on earth is that noise?" Ruth said.

The boy's chest was clenched like a fist, his eyes watering, the lack of air making his head whirl. Samuel stood, knocking the chair over, and banged down on the table.

Ruth twisted around. She saw the boy's face, bright red, and the terror in his eyes. She hesitated, just for a moment, as if she were not sure what to do. Then she shouted, "Samuel!"

The housekeeper ran across the kitchen, pushing the boy forward, and then pounded on his back. Samuel's eyes had fogged up and his head was a vault of pressure and pain. Ruth struck his back again, causing his body to flatten out on the table. She hit him again and then again.

He was going to vomit. That's what it felt like. Then something shot up and a river of blood and sick spilled across the kitchen table. Samuel took a greedy breath and began to cough.

"Thank God for that." Ruth kept her hand at his back. "Mercy."

Samuel took another breath and then another, wiping his mouth and then his eyes, which were foggy with tears.

"Are you all right?" Ruth picked up the chair and eased him down.

"I couldn't breathe. I was choking."

Ruth fetched him a glass of water. "The cake must have gone down the wrong way."

Samuel could taste the bitterness of blood in his mouth. He pointed to the pool of vomit on the table. "It wasn't the cake."

Ruth looked down and saw in among the bile an object roughly the size of a raisin, slick with blood. She picked it up and held it to the window.

"What is it?" said Samuel.

"Glass." Ruth said this faintly. "It's a piece of glass."

Before Samuel could ask how a piece of glass had found its way into the chocolate cake, Ruth went over and washed it under the tap, then placed it down on the table. She said, "I dropped the jug of cream when I was making the cake—it hit the edge of the table and shattered. I thought all of the pieces went on the floor but . . ."

The water trembled in Samuel's hand as he took a drink and the cool liquid felt like fire rushing down his throat.

"Butter fingers, that's what I've got." Ruth's face was a web of frowns. She stood over him, had him open his mouth. "Does it hurt?"

"Just my throat."

"There's some bleeding but I don't see any serious damage." She leaned closer still, her stale breath hitting his face like a warm breeze. "I'll ring for Dr. Wolfe if you like." Then she put her hand under the boy's chin. "It's up to you, of course, but he's such a nosy one and I'm just concerned that he might find other things needing his attention besides your throat."

Samuel swallowed and the pain buckled his face. "Like what?"

"Well, as I was saying, you've been so troubled of late, one look at you and he'll see that, and then he might ask questions and, well, I just don't want him hearing all the ghastly things you've been thinking about—murder and wickedness. He's sure to think your mind is disordered and he'd want to do all kinds of tests, probably at one of those hospitals in London, and after that, I don't want to think about what would become of you. I'd do my best to tell him it's just that you miss your mother and that all these shocking thoughts are the result of a wild imagination, but doctors rarely listen to people like me." She smiled but her heart wasn't in it. "I'm sure your throat will mend itself just fine, but if you want me to call Dr. Wolfe, I'll do it right now. It's up to you, Samuel."

Samuel shook his head. "Don't call him."

Ruth let her hand drop from his chin. "As you wish."

"I need to change my clothes." Samuel was looking down at the blood and sick on his shirt and trousers.

"You stink to high heaven." Ruth got a cloth and ran it under the tap. "Why don't you take a bath while I clean this mess up?"

"All right."

"I'll make you some tea with honey—that'll do wonders for your throat."

Samuel stood up. He tasted the blood rising up in his mouth and forced himself to swallow. "Thank you, Ruth."

23

The atlas glowed under the lamplight. Samuel was seated at the small table, his arms crossed, his head resting on his hands, his eyes traveling between Boston and West Cornwall. The lamp sprayed soft orange light over the white pages, causing them to flare and shimmer like sand dunes in the desert. The pages were curved just a little at the spine and the blue of the water between England and America seemed to swell with dark promise. Was his mother on a ship right now sailing that ocean back home to him? He'd had such hopes before and been left feeling foolish—wasn't the tiny wooden tugboat sitting statically in the middle of the Atlantic Ocean proof of his stupidity? He looked at the red yarn tethered to the boat and followed its tail, snaking back to the web of pins marking all the places his mother had visited. Wanting a thing had no power to summon it.

The boy's throat hurt a great deal but the bleeding had nearly stopped. His mouth still tasted bitter and sickly but the worst of the headache had passed. He'd taken a bath just like Ruth told him to. She came in with the tea and took up a sponge, scrubbing the bile from his face and neck. She talked the whole time, which wasn't usually her way, about every little thing—how much shortbread and cake she hoped to sell at the market on Saturday, about the exorbitant cost of good cheese and what William should do in the garden next (the hedge along the front fence). Every now and then she would stop and ask Samuel if he was all right and he would always tell her that he was.

"You're not saying much of anything," Ruth had said.

Samuel would just shrug. "I'm tired."

"Well, that's to be expected."

After the bath, Samuel had gone down to the kitchen to get himself a glass of milk. Ruth claimed that, second only to her honey tea, it was just the thing for his throat. So the boy had taken her advice. Well, that was his story, anyway. Really, he wanted to make sure Ruth was occupied cooking the pork pie for dinner so he could steal away. By then the sun had all but fallen, and when he'd walked into his mother's study, the bay window practically sang to him. So that's where he went, standing there, watching the dusk light up behind the trees in the back garden, a mottled wound of red and purple. It was hard not to miss her the most then.

They would think you were a very sick boy, because a healthy mind wouldn't harbor such dark thoughts. Ruth's words nested inside of him. *You would be taken from this house and put*

in a hospital and you might never come back.
Was his mind troubled? He'd never considered
the possibility. He didn't always think terrible
thoughts, but lately, Samuel couldn't pretend he
hadn't imagined the very worst things.

He wanted to have a healthy mind; he wanted
to be like any other boy. What would his mother
think if she came home and he was in a hospital
for children who had gone mad? He knew she
would find that a great burden. She would think
he was disordered, afflicted in the worst way,
and she might never want him near her again.
The risk was very real and he couldn't pretend
otherwise.

Samuel felt the pull of the atlas and what was
hidden there. He had sat down at the desk, his
eyes level with the map, and gazed longingly at
the pins marking his mother's travels. Had he
gone mad? And if he had, how could a madman
know for certain?

Ruth said he had horrible thoughts about
ghastly things. True enough. When he caught
her going through his mother's drawer, he hadn't
wanted to believe that she was really looking for
her lost clover pin. He'd thought it was proof
she had done something awful. His mind wanted
him to think that. And, just that afternoon, hadn't
he had dark thoughts about that piece of glass?
Didn't it occur to him, right after Ruth said the
jug had broken, that perhaps she'd put the piece

of glass in the cake on purpose? His mind wanted him to doubt her, to recall how angry she was when he mentioned her pa and after what Mrs. Collins had said about the dead bodies piled up in the cellar. To wonder if this was her way of punishing him. Or even killing him. And to remember that moment when Ruth had hesitated, just for a second, after she saw him choking.

These were all terrible thoughts, hinting at something tangled and rotten. Dr. Wolfe would know there was something wrong with him just by looking at him, that's what Ruth said. Samuel knew he had to stop thinking bad things. His mother was in America, but just like Ruth said, she would soon be home. Nothing was wrong. He had her postcards, the ones where she said how much she was missing him. Wasn't that proof enough?

Though she might be hundreds of miles away, Samuel warmed to the idea that in a way she was closer than that. For a part of her was hidden in the pages of the atlas. He hadn't wanted to finish her letter because she had written that she didn't want Samuel to visit her while she was resting up in Bath. Samuel's sickly mind wanted him to think that this meant something awful, that it meant she didn't want him near her. But if he could summon the courage to revisit the letter he was sure it would show that his mother loved him very much, and if she hadn't wanted him to visit her, well, there must have been a very good reason. So the boy peeled back the pages of the atlas, careful not to disturb the pins and yarn, and pulled out the envelope wedged between a map of the Antarctic.

He held the envelope and listened for any sound of footsteps. All was silent. Samuel pulled out the letter and went straight to the second page, his eyes swimming across the opulent scrawl until he found what he was looking for.

When you write and tell me how much Samuel misses me and how he cries for me, it only makes things worse. If you only knew how wretched I feel when he is clinging to me and calling for me over and over. I feel as if I cannot breathe, my darling. I feel as if I am being pulled under the waves and that I am so far down not even you can reach me.

Samuel stopped and his eyes flew back to where he had started. He read the sentences again, trying his best to understand them. He wasn't sure what the waves had to do with anything but he felt confident the rest of it was well within his grasp. His mother wanted so much to be there for him that sometimes it took the breath right from out of her. Yes, that's what it was. Her love for him was so great it sometimes made her feel as if she were sinking.

That was why she did not want Samuel to visit her. Because she knew that seeing him would excite her so and wear her out, which is not smart when you are supposed to be resting. With a faint smile, Samuel turned the page and read on.

There are days when it is all I can do not to run away. Please don't think me a monster but sometimes I actually plan it out in my head— where I would go and what my life would be like. It's not that I don't love our life together; it is just that all around us are problems.

Married life is not all bliss. Please don't think that I expect it to be.

All I ask is that you allow me to be a part of things. I know you wish to keep our financial strife to yourself— you are trying to protect me from our troubles—but have you ever thought that I might be able to help?

It seems that the only role you have in mind for me is the one I am not suited for. You have a better way with him than I ever could—it seems so natural and so easy between the

two of you that I sometimes resent you both for it. Can you understand, my darling? I do so want to love

Samuel pinched his fingers to turn the page. But page three didn't give way to the next, for there was no next page. He went through the letter again. Page one, page two, page three. He felt each page carefully—perhaps page four was stuck behind one of the other sheets. It wasn't. The boy reread the last paragraph, a frown carved like a scar between his eyes, and after a while the words became a blur and it was hard to make any sense of them.

He didn't understand, not in any way that felt good; he just knew that his mother was unhappy. And that the next page of that letter was very important. What was she trying to say? Was she writing about him? Samuel's wicked mind began to play with him again but he did his best to chase the thoughts away.

She loved him. She loved him best of all and he could prove it, too. All he needed was the rest of that letter. That would clear everything up, because she was certain to have written something special about him in closing—wasn't that usually when the most tender feelings are put down on paper? The missing page was probably mixed up with the other letters in his mother's bedroom. Samuel folded the letter and returned it to the Antarctic. Then he went to the desk drawer and pulled out the key.

"Samuel!" Ruth's voice was like a bark in the night. "Where have you gotten to?"

"I'm in here," Samuel called back. He listened for footsteps but heard none.

"Where's here?"

"Mother's study."

"Whatever for?"

"Just looking at the atlas."

"Well, your dinner's ready, so hurry along."

Samuel closed the drawer, slipped the key into his pocket and set off toward the kitchen.

24

"How's that throat?"

"The bleeding's stopped," said Samuel.

"Didn't I tell you it would?"

Samuel nodded. "It still hurts, though."

"Be gone by the morning, you mark my words."

After dinner, if Ruth was in a good mood, they sometimes had tea or hot chocolate in the sitting room. Ruth liked to listen to the radio, usually some sort of detective story or a quiz show, where very smart people would answer questions. Often, Ruth would know the answer before the smart people and Samuel had told her more than once that she should go on one of those shows and win the prizes. Ruth would always wave him off and say that she was no scholar, and besides, who ever heard of a housekeeper winning a quiz show?

Samuel took another sip of hot chocolate. The fire in the hearth was little more than kindling, and as the boy watched the smoldering logs begin to crumble, it didn't hold his interest the way it usually did. He was thinking about how he might slip away and find the missing pages of that letter and he understood it wouldn't be easily managed.

Typically, Ruth was everywhere all at once, but lately it was even worse—as if her eyes were always upon him. She was either passing by or coming to find him or looking from afar. She seemed to know where he was headed before he did. Twice, Samuel had said he needed to use the toilet upstairs and twice Ruth had said the one downstairs was just as good so he should use that one instead. Yes, it would take some managing.

"Did you finish writing the psalm?" Ruth had her reading glasses on and was mending a hole in one of Samuel's favorite shirts.

"Yes." Samuel shrugged. "Well, almost."

"You were to finish it today." Ruth looked at Samuel from over the top of her glasses, which was her way of conveying utter seriousness. "Was I not clear about that?"

"I was going to work on it after school but then . . ."

But then he had nearly choked to death on a piece of glass. A piece of glass that Ruth had baked into a chocolate cake. This wasn't said aloud but it splashed about between the silence, which is why Ruth sniffed and her voice lost some of its edge. "Well, I don't suppose the day is over yet." She looked down at her watch. "You've still got forty-five minutes until bedtime. Fetch the Bible and finish it now."

"But Revered Pryce isn't coming to class until Monday."

"Even so, it's best you get it done now."

Suddenly a solution rose up in front of Samuel.

He got out of his chair and started toward the door. "You're right, I should get it finished. Good night, Ruth."

"Good night?" Ruth was looking at him over her glasses again. "And just why are you wishing me a good night?"

"The Bible's in my bedroom."

"What on earth is it doing there? Isn't it in the kitchen?"

It was in the kitchen. But Samuel knew he had to push on. "I took it up after dinner, so that I could work on it before bed."

Ruth seemed to consider this for a moment, her eyes closing to a squint. Finally, she said, "Well, go up and get it, then."

"Shouldn't I finish it in my room?" Samuel motioned to the radio sitting between two armchairs. "It might be very distracting."

"Nonsense." Ruth held the shirt up to the lamp and examined her stitching. "I'll turn the radio down if I must. Besides, I want to be sure you write the Queen's English in such a way that Reverend Pryce will be able to read it."

This was unhelpful, but Samuel would have to make do. "Yes, Ruth."

He checked the clock by the radio and then walked quickly into the hall.

He wanted to run up the stairs but Ruth would probably have something to say about that. She hated running on the stairs. Said it sounded like a stampede and made her head rattle. So Samuel took two at a time and went as fast as he could manage without stomping on the boards.

When he got up to the landing, the grandfather clock's wretched tick seemed to delight in reminding him he didn't have much time. He had to break into his mother's bedroom, find the missing pages of the letter, then steal into the kitchen, get the Bible and his workbook and make it back into the sitting room without rousing Ruth's suspicions. There was hardly any time, but right at that moment, finding the rest of the letter felt like the only way to chase away the wicked thoughts and make things better.

Coming off the landing, Samuel began to run. He didn't pay any mind to the grim shadows splayed about the corridor and he barely noticed that the moonlight drifting through the windows had drenched the long, empty corridor in a kind of mist. As he came to a halt outside his mother's door he was already digging the key out of his pocket.

The door opened and the boy rushed into the bedroom, tripping on the rug and nearly crashing to the floor. The curtains were drawn, and Samuel had to feel along the wall to find the lamp. He switched it on and then jumped over the bed, moving swiftly toward the object of his attention.

The top drawer opened roughly, catching on the

left side. The baby blanket was folded neatly and everything else looked undisturbed. Samuel just assumed the contents of the drawer would be in a great mess after Ruth had been in there looking for her pin. But everything was neatly arranged and in its proper place. He lifted out his father's baby blanket and placed it on top of the chest and then searched through its folds for the slim parcel of letters. They weren't there.

Samuel didn't want the bad thoughts, but they clawed at him, anyway. All about Ruth removing those letters so that Samuel wouldn't know what his mother had written. No, he reminded himself, she had been looking for her pin, nothing more. Just looking for her pin, which meant so much to her because her father, God rest his soul, had given it to her. The letters must be there; he just had to keep looking. He pulled out the rusted tea tin with his mother's gold earrings and the ruby necklace in it, placing it on top of the blanket. Under it was a stack of wrapping paper covered in white and red stripes and to the left were an address book and a volume of poetry by someone called Wordsworth. Samuel moved them aside and found that under these things was his bounty.

The boy untied the parcel of letters. There were four in total. The fifth was hidden in the atlas down in his mother's study. Samuel glanced at the clock on the mantel—he'd been gone eight minutes. Ruth would soon be looking for him if she wasn't already. Still, he had to find those missing pages.

His hands worked quickly, opening each of the letters. They were all addressed to his father, from the same address in Bath, and though the words flew past him in a blur there was hardly a mention of his name, just a great deal about the hot springs and her reinvigorated spirits and Dr. Boyle. What he didn't find was the fourth page. How could it have vanished into thin air? It had to be there somewhere; pages from important letters don't just disappear.

There wasn't time to think on this. Samuel eyed the clock again. Ten minutes.

"Samuel, what are you doing up there?"

It sounded like Ruth was in the hall, probably at the bottom of the stairs.

"Coming, Ruth!" Samuel yelled back. "I had to go to the toilet again."

"Did you indeed? Well, just get yourself down here and finish that infernal psalm."

"Yes, Ruth."

Samuel put the letters back where he found them. After all, they were no good to him, and besides, Ruth might check. Next, he took the tea tin and placed it at the bottom of the drawer and then covered it over with the blanket. His hands were moving faster than his mind, so it took a moment for him to realize. That's when he stopped. Samuel set the blanket aside again and picked up the tea tin once more. The one with his mother's very favorite jewels in it—the earrings from her wedding day and the necklace his father had given to her when Samuel was born. He picked it up, even though he had no time, for one reason only. The tin hadn't rattled. It hadn't released its distorted percussion, the clack and clatter of the jewels moving about inside it.

"Samuel Clay, do I have to come up there and get you myself?" shouted Ruth.

"Coming!"

Samuel unscrewed the lid and looked inside, and the dark void he found there, full of nothing but questions, made the bad thoughts dance anew before his eyes.

25

The devil didn't come looking for him. Samuel expected to hear her stomping down the corridor, almost certainly with a look of thunder on her face. But it didn't happen. He'd put everything back in the drawer, locked the bedroom door and hurried down the back stairs to collect the Bible and workbook from the kitchen.

He flew down the narrow steps and along the back passageway, leading straight into the kitchen. Ruth was a nasty crook, he knew that now. She had stolen his mother's best jewels. That's what he had caught her doing the other day when she was going through the drawer—stealing like a rotten, no-good robber. It was just as Joseph had said: Ruth was up to no good. And if she was wicked enough to steal his mother's jewels right from her very own bedroom, then was it really so hard to believe she could do much worse? Ruth had hurt his mother; didn't that empty tea tin practically shout that out? She was the reason his mother had vanished in the night. She was why his mother hadn't come back in over one hundred and nineteen days. Ruth was the devil.

He would confront her about the missing jewels—he knew he must—but then she would know he had done the very thing she told him not to do and then it wouldn't be about the stolen earrings and the necklace; it would be about what a horrible boy Samuel was for breaking into his mother's bedroom. Ruth had a way of doing that. He wouldn't let her twist and turn things around on him this time. She killed his mother. And she had put that glass in the chocolate cake to kill him, too.

Ruth thought herself very clever. She'd probably plotted this whole thing out, dreaming of having the house to herself and his mother's jewels besides. Just like that housekeeper in Germany. But Ruth wasn't as smart as she imagined. Samuel knew what she'd been up to and she wouldn't get away with it. He would do something terrible to her: smash her in the head with a hammer and let her bleed to death or push her down the stairs and listen as her bones broke and her neck snapped. He would kill her for what she'd done. Wouldn't his mother be looking down from the other side and wouldn't she want him to avenge her? To make Ruth pay for taking her away from him and for being a cold-blooded murderer and a no-good thief? It would take some thinking about, some planning and such, but he would do it.

The kitchen was wrapped in layers of twilight, the cupboards vanishing into the gloom, the large table rendered an ominous black box. Samuel squinted to make something out of the darkness, moving swiftly in the direction of the icebox. Despite the rage in his heart, he couldn't deny there was fear pulsing there. If Ruth caught him she would know the Bible hadn't been in his bedroom and that he had lied.

Samuel's right elbow hit the icebox. He reached out and felt around it for his schoolbook and the Bible. He couldn't find them. And he knew, he just knew, what that meant.

"Looking for something?"

Ruth's voice seemed to blow at him like a cold wind.

He blinked into the darkness. "Ruth?"

The light came on and she was there, standing by the door, the Bible in her hand. Her face looked remarkably smooth in the pale light, her eyes two dark pools, her mouth almost carved into a half grin. Samuel didn't want to be afraid. She had done awful things—he knew that now—and what he owed her was fury not fear. Yet he did fear her. He was afraid.

"Do you think me a stupid woman?" Ruth was looking at him as if she were reading a book she didn't quite understand. "Is that it, Samuel? You think it's as easy as telling me a story and then getting up to no good while I sit downstairs like a fool mending your clothes? Is that how it is?"

"No, Ruth."

"But isn't that just what I've caught you doing?" Ruth uttered this softly, looking down at

182

the Bible. "Lying to me about where this is and then going upstairs?"

Samuel couldn't think what to say.

Ruth was shaking her head now. "There isn't anything you can do that I won't know about, Samuel. This house won't hold your secrets— it will betray them. In every creak of the floorboards, every foot on the back stairs, every flick of a light switch, every turn of a key—this house tells its tales for anyone with sense enough to listen."

"I thought the Bible was upstairs."

"Oh, yes?" Ruth was leaning against the door-frame. "So it's not that you lied to my face? It's that you just thought you had taken it to your room? You just *imagined* doing something you never did? Is that the sorry tale you're asking me to believe?"

Samuel nodded his head. Ruth's cool indignation was a beast with many heads, many weapons, and it made easy work of snuffing out his own righteous anger. He might have imagined that knowing what she had done would arm him against her. But now he saw that while she was a general, battle-scarred and fearless, he was hardly a foot soldier.

"I won't allow you to wallow in the foul waters of deceit." Ruth's voice had found its muscle again. "Some sort of degenerate who tells a lie as easily as tying their shoelaces. I won't have it,

Samuel Clay." She lifted her finger and beckoned him. "Come here."

The telephone's shrill ring took them both by surprise. Ruth glanced out into the hall and then back at Samuel. And that was all the boy needed. He ran for the back stairs.

26

"Get back here!" Ruth shouted. "Now, Samuel!"

The ferocity was there, in every hollered word, but something else was there, too. Samuel was well schooled in the timbre of her rage, so he heard that tiny pocket, that small pinprick, of hesitation.

Ruth never could let a telephone go unanswered. He was running along the second-story landing when the telephone stilled and he heard Ruth's voice rising up from the hall below. Samuel crouched down, a safe distance from the banister.

"That does sound exciting," Ruth was saying. "I expect you meet a lot of very interesting characters at gatherings like that . . . Oh, would I? Perhaps I'm not as easily shocked as you might think." Ruth laughed then and it sounded sincere. She was twisting the cord around her fingers and swaying just a little. "No, Mr. Clay, still no word on Mrs. Clay's return."

Mr. Clay? That was his father's name, but he had gone to an eternal rest or was watching from the other side. The small cloud of confusion quickly parted and Samuel realized that Ruth must be talking to his uncle Felix. That made the boy lean forward, straining to listen.

"Yes, well, I don't need to tell you about Mrs. Clay." Ruth's voice practically sang with condemnation. "She never likes being tied down for long." Silence. "Exactly."

Hearing this caused the boy's teeth to clench, his nostrils to flare. Ruth was lying about his mother, making it seem like she wanted to be away, when all the while *she* was the reason his mother wasn't there. Samuel stood up.

"Oh, we're managing well enough," Ruth went on. "Well, I won't pretend things aren't tight but, as I say, we're managing." There was a pause. "I'm afraid Samuel's at a friend's house. It's the boy's birthday and he invited Samuel to stay the night."

Samuel was running down the stairs. He had to talk to Uncle Felix—tell him everything and make him call the police and get them to come and take Ruth to prison. To the gallows. The housekeeper glanced up and saw him on the stairs.

"Yes, Mr. Clay." Her words were tumbling out now. "I'll be sure to tell him. You have a lovely time at your little soiree."

Samuel jumped the last three steps and broke into a sprint.

"Good night to you, sir."

His hand swung through the air, grasping for the telephone, but Ruth slammed it down. Such was Samuel's speed that he stumbled over her and hit the table, knocking the receiver from its perch. It dropped to the floor with a clang.

Ruth bent down and calmly returned the receiver to its rightful place. "I thought you'd disgraced yourself enough for one night, but you're outdoing yourself, Samuel."

The boy's hands were on his hips, his breaths rapid. "That was Uncle Felix and don't say it wasn't."

"Why would I?" Ruth patted her hair.

"I want to talk to him. I'm going to tell him all about you."

"Are you?"

Samuel reached for the phone, snatching it up. "I'll ring him right now."

"Go ahead. He's wasn't calling from home." Ruth looked unbearably superior.

Samuel frowned; he couldn't help it. "Where is he?"

"That's none of your concern."

"He rang to speak to me."

"Don't be ridiculous." Ruth sighed. "He was asking after your mother."

"I heard everything." The fear had fallen away and the anger swept Samuel up, giving him the courage to look her in the eye. "You were right, Ruth, this house will tell you its secrets if you listen carefully enough. You told Uncle Felix I wasn't here. You are the one who lies as easily as tying your shoelaces!"

If Ruth was shocked by his boldness she didn't show it.

"Can you blame me for that?" She met Samuel's glare, and if the boy hadn't known better, he might have thought she was regarding him with heartfelt pity. "Your mind is afflicted, Samuel, and it seems to get worse by the day. Lord only knows what your uncle would make of the madness coming out of your mouth. Do you suppose I could protect you from his good intentions? You would be put away and I couldn't do a thing to stop it."

"I am not sick."

"Oh, but you are. How else can you explain it? Does a well child deceive and sneak about? Does a well child listen at doors in the dead of night? Does a well child ring his uncle and whisper about murderous conspiracies? Oh, yes, I know all about that. And finally, does a well child truly believe his mother has been chopped up in the cellar?"

Ruth's words could hollow out just about any certainty and they had felled Samuel more times than he could count. The idea that he was ill—that his mind was sickly and that he was imagining things that weren't so—was a powerful one. It might have stilled the urgent voice in his head if not for one very important thing.

"The tea tin," said Samuel softly.

This caused Ruth to scowl. "The what?"

"Mother's tea tin." Samuel stepped toward her. "The one that had her very best jewels in it. The earrings from when she married Father and the ruby necklace he gave her when I was born."

She understood now and it played upon her face.

"They were there just a few days ago," Samuel said, "and now they're gone."

"How would you know what was or wasn't in your mother's bedroom? That door is locked." It was just like Ruth to cling to one small part of this, grasping it tightly.

Samuel dug the key out of his pocket and let it fall onto the floor. What use was it now? "You took those jewels, Ruth. You weren't looking for your pin, were you? It was Mother's necklace and earrings you were after."

"I did lose my pin, whether you want to believe it or not. As for the jewelry . . ." Samuel waited for her to deny it or turn things around and accuse him of being the thief. But she didn't. Instead, she said, "I took them."

"You stole them! They don't belong to you and you stole them!"

The soft light coming from the sitting room caused Ruth's hair to flare and flicker. "Why do I bake so much shortbread?"

The boy's eyes narrowed to a slit. What did

that have to do with anything? She was trying to confuse him and he wouldn't let her.

"Why do I bake hundreds of shortbread every week?" said Ruth again. "I'm asking you a question, Samuel."

"You sell them at the market," said Samuel sharply. "What has that got to do with—?"

"And why do you suppose the head house-keeper of such a fine home is going to the market every Saturday and selling shortbread and cake like some sort of penniless widow?"

Samuel refused to answer her.

"It's the same reason I had to let Olive go and why I can't pay William his wages or the butcher's bill. The money your mother left when she sailed for America is gone. I've hardly two pennies to rub together and the only way I can put food on the table is by selling what I bake at the market. There's bills and expenses . . . this is a grand house but there's no money to keep it running."

The story Ruth was trying to weave was plain enough, but Samuel wouldn't let her wrap the tale around him. "You stole from my mother."

"I did no such thing!" Ruth was shouting and her voice repeated all the way up to the domed ceiling. "Before your mother went away, she showed me where those jewels were hidden and left me the key to her door." She glanced down at what was lying by Samuel's feet. "The only key, or so I thought. She said if the money she left ran out, I was to sell those jewels."

"You're lying!" Samuel's words echoed just the same as Ruth's had, which was reassuring. "Mother loved those jewels best of all. She told me so a hundred times and she has all kinds of other necklaces and rings and earrings. Why wouldn't she sell those instead of the ones Father had given her?"

"Because they're all gone, Samuel. Your mother sold almost everything last year after your father died. There was so much debt and your grandfather wouldn't help. I'm sure you've noticed the vases and paintings and all the rest vanishing—here one day, gone the next. You're right, your mother loved the necklace and earrings best of all. That's why she left them until last. But when it's money you need, things matter a lot less. And when you sell them, it's not because you want to, but because there's simply no other choice."

What Ruth was saying sounded true enough. Things had gone missing all over the house, Olive had been let go and William was complaining about his wages. Samuel had known about the troubles with money for some time and his mother never hid it from him. Sometimes it felt like that was all that she could talk about. And she was often away, visiting the steel mill in Lincolnshire or traveling all over to try and raise capital.

So it made sense now. Why Ruth was in his mother's bedroom churning through the drawer—she had been looking for the tin. But did that make her innocent? How was Samuel to know whether his mother had given Ruth permission to take those jewels? All he had was her word and what was that worth? Hadn't she lied to stop him talking to Uncle Felix? Ruth said it was because Uncle Felix would know that Samuel was unwell, that he had a sickly mind, but he didn't believe that. Ruth had done some awful things. His throat still burned from the glass he had swallowed. Glass that Ruth had baked into that cake, which was chocolate and his very favorite because she had wanted him to eat it, practically ordering him to gobble it down. And she hesitated, didn't she? Right when she should have been running to help him, Ruth had looked over and . . . just stood there. That pause didn't last for more than a second or two but he had seen it and he knew what it meant.

"You tried to kill me." He was nodding. "You wanted me to choke on that glass."

Ruth reached down and picked up the key. "It's been a trying night and I think we're both ready for bed. You may finish the psalm in the morning."

It was as if he hadn't spoken. That was the worst part.

Samuel thought of his mother, murdered at

Ruth's hand, and he wanted the hate to glisten in his eyes. "Joseph was right about everything. You killed my mother. You killed—"

She moved swiftly, her hand flying out and catching his neck, pushing him against the wall. She squeezed his throat and Samuel's fingers gripped her wrist, trying to pull her away. Then she looked at the tension in her hand, the plump veins, and it was as if she remembered herself. Her grip slackened and Samuel's head snapped forward. He took a gasp of air, just as Ruth's hand slid down his chest and held him there. She was pressed close to him, her lips finding his ear. "I don't want things to get unpleasant, I never do, but repeat that again and you'll learn what I am capable of."

Samuel tried to get away but her hand was unmoving.

"I know you aren't well," she whispered, "and I am trying to be merciful, but there are limits to what I will take and that is where we find ourselves. Perhaps I should call the doctor and let him decide what should be done with you. That mind of yours is turning against you, Samuel Clay, and I fear you're beyond my reach now."

Ruth released her hold and pressed the key into his hand. "Put this back where you found it and take yourself up to bed."

She walked slowly from the hall, patting down

her hair and making a sound that might have been an unhurried sigh. It drifted around the great hall like faraway music, and as Samuel stood there, shaking and catching his breath, he would almost swear that she was humming.

27

Waiting was the worst part. He knew Ruth would come to check on him, she always did, making sure he was tucked up in bed like he was supposed to be and wishing him a stern goodnight. Samuel lay on his back, trying to arrange everything in his mind so it made sense. Ruth had done something awful to his mother, probably killed her, and she now knew that Samuel had figured it out. That's why she put the glass in the chocolate cake. To get rid of him before he told anyone else. He wasn't the one with the sickly mind. It was her. She was manic, a cold-blooded killer, and she meant to get rid of him so she could have the house to herself.

This certainty wasn't without its problems. Samuel's father used to say that when you find one wrong thing in an ocean of right, it's like a fly in the ointment. The postcards were the fly in the ointment—the one thing that raised doubt about Ruth's guilt. They had come from America and they were written in his mother's handwriting, the boy couldn't deny that. Joseph said Ruth might know someone in America, a coconspirator, who was sending the cards for her. But how would that person know what his mother's handwriting looked like?

Samuel flinched as he swallowed, his throat still aching. He would call the police and tell them about Ruth. Surely they would be able to help him. They would know his mother hadn't abandoned him with a monster like Ruth. That she hadn't just left him there, while she went off to America to meet with those toffee-nosed bankers. They would know that something was wrong and that Ruth had done a dreadful thing to keep his mother away from him for all this time.

Tears pooled in his eyes, spilling over, but he chased them away, grateful for the darkness. He wasn't sad, he was angry, and that anger made his lips press tight together and his hands ball into fists. Everything was wrong and it was all Ruth's fault. His rage had another source, too. Samuel knew that he had no proof. His mother wasn't in the cellar or the woodshed. And everyone believed Ruth and her beastly lies. Mrs. Collins was the worst of them. She had laughed with Ruth about his mother being stabbed and her body hidden away. She thought it was the funniest thing, the silliest thing, she ever heard.

The police would be the same, wouldn't they? They'd probably laugh just like Mrs. Collins. What Samuel needed was proof, real proof, and luckily he knew where to get it. Hadn't he seen Ruth through the keyhole, all hunched over, writing furiously? Joseph guessed that Ruth kept a diary in which she spelled out all her murderous deeds. The rightness of this theory sat in Samuel now like an old friend. Ruth was just the type and that diary would read like a confession. All he had to do was get hold of it and then everyone would know what she had done to his beautiful mother, gone one hundred and nineteen days.

The minutes slipped by and Ruth didn't come to check on him. Though his mind was a gale and his heart raged, in time, the angels of sleep drifted down and reached out their hands for him. His eyes had grown heavy by then, and though it wasn't the time, the boy found there was no other choice than to reach back.

The landing above the hall rippled with morning light. It streamed in through the windows and poured across the wooden floors; even the walls were a shimmering gold and the marble pillars seemed to heave and swell, as if the sun was pouring into them. The light was so blinding, so impossibly golden, Samuel needed his hand to shield his eyes.

He had seen her from his bedroom window, that's why he was running toward the landing. He didn't remember getting up, but he must have, and then wandered over to the window. That's when he spotted her walking toward the house. So he ran all the way; his hand barely touched the banister as he came down the stairs.

The front door was open, sunlight flooding in

like a fog, and when it cleared, Samuel looked down and saw her floating into the hall as if on a breeze. She was wearing her favorite yellow dress with the ivy around the trim and her bags were clustered on the black-and-white checkered floor. She spotted him and her smile was magnificent. "It's such a glorious morning," she told him, "I decided to walk from the station." Then she threw her arms out, her eyes only for him. "Oh, how I've missed my little man."

They hugged for the longest time, neither one of them wanting to let go. She smelled of lilies and mint and he could hear her crying and it was all because she had missed him dreadfully and was so happy to be home. Then she pulled back and held his face tenderly in her hands.

"Samuel." His mother's bright smile began to dim. "Samuel?"

Her hand slipped down to his shoulders and she started to shake him, her plump red lips faded to a thin line. "Samuel!"

His eyes fluttered open and he squinted, putting a hand up to his eyes. Through the web of his fingers he could see her, sitting on the edge of his bed, the soft light from the bedside lamp bleeding across her face.

"I'm sorry to wake you," said Ruth, though she didn't sound sorry at all. "I didn't want to leave things as they were." She sighed and closed her eyes briefly. "We seem to be bringing out the worst in each other lately and it can't continue, now can it?"

Ruth was dressed in her robe and Samuel wondered if she was ill—her eyes were bloated, and while some of her hair was still twisted in a bun, long strands hung loose about her face. "Samuel, you mustn't give in to the sickness in your mind. You must be stronger than these wicked thoughts whispering to you of murder and wrongdoing."

Ruth was leaning close to his face; her breath was hot with an acridness the boy thought might be vinegar. He presumed she had been sleeping because her words came out sluggishly and her eyes would close without warning and then spring open like she'd just had a fright.

"I know the root of this problem, yes, indeed." She waved her finger in front of Samuel's face. "It's that Joseph Collins who first put this nonsense into your head and don't even try to deny it."

Samuel would have defended his best and only friend, but before he could, Ruth was talking again.

"He's a fool without a bit of common sense and shame on you for believing a word that comes out of his mouth. Is he responsible for that foolishness about the cellar?"

Samuel shook his head.

"Well, I don't believe you, and I'm sure he's

also the reason you were snooping in the wood-shed the other day." Ruth saw the look of panic flash across Samuel's face and nodded. "Oh, yes, William told me all about that. He thought it was hysterical, you poking about looking for buried treasure or some such thing. I hadn't the stomach to tell him what you were really looking for." Ruth rubbed her chin as if she had a great itch. "Deep down, Samuel, deep down inside you must know what's true. You can't really believe I could . . . that I murdered your mother?"

The boy pictured his mother, as she had been in the dream, in her yellow dress, the sun all around her, so happy to be home. And he knew that it would never happen. "Yes."

"I see." She sniffed. "Then tell me this, Samuel. Why did I do it? Why on earth would I have done such a thing? Your mother's never been anything but fair and kind to me."

Normally when Ruth asked Samuel a question he would look inside of himself for the very thing that would upset her the least. But the *right* words, the ones she was hoping on, just wouldn't come and all he was left with was the truth. "You murdered Mother because she was going to fire you."

Ruth gasped, though she was smirking. "Was she now? Might I ask why she was firing me?"

"The money's all gone. Olive had to be let go and Mother was letting you go, too, and you got very angry and did something, and maybe you didn't even mean to do it, but you did and then you had to hide the awful truth or else you would hang."

"Let us say you're right. Let us say your mother was going to let me go. Then what? Was she to take care of this house, clean and cook, look after you, and at the same time save the steel mill, not to mention keep it running?" Her eyes fluttered shut again. "Did you ever see your mother so much as boil an egg?"

Samuel hadn't.

"You know well enough that she could hardly stay in one spot for more than a minute." Ruth yawned and didn't even cover her mouth. "I want you to think, really think, Samuel. Would your mother have let me go? The one person who keeps this house running so she is free to go where she pleases at the drop of a hat?"

Samuel couldn't deny the sense in all of that. But it didn't mean Ruth was any less wicked. "Perhaps you do everything around here because you love this house," he said. "You love it so much that you want it all for yourself and that's why you killed Mother."

"Nonsense," said Ruth with a soft chuckle.

"And you took Mother's jewels so that you could swan around like Lady Muck."

"Lady Muck?" She huffed. "Those jewels were taken to a man in Penzance while you were at school. He'll send them on to London, where we'll get the best price."

She had an answer for everything and that only made his mother feel farther away and harder to find. Samuel could feel that he was on the very brink of tears.

"You're a bad woman."

Ruth's hand came up and pushed the hair from his eyes. "I know what it's like to fret for someone and wish with every part of you that they'd come back. My pa went away." She shook her head like she was cross with herself. "No, not away. Died, that's what he did. I wasn't much older than you when it happened."

Samuel didn't want to care about Ruth or her stupid father—but there were some things that practically cried out for answers, even from a scoundrel like Ruth.

"How did he die?"

"He was a blacksmith, a fine one, too, but he never could be happy. He tried—he looked for it all over—but even when he found it, he never could hold it for long."

Talking of happiness like it was a thing to be found and held didn't make a great deal of sense to Samuel.

"Pa would stay in bed for days sometimes or he'd go off somewhere and come back a week later even glummer than when he left." Ruth shrugged and Samuel saw that her eyes were slick with what he guessed was sorrow. "It's a terrible thing when a person gets worn down by life and decides it's not for them. Pa had tried once before . . ."

Samuel wasn't clear what he had tried once before but he supposed it wasn't anything good.

"It was summer and he'd stopped working, stopped everything. Ma did what she could to keep things running along—took in washing and cleaned houses for people in town. She was gone most days and she put me in charge of Pa." Ruth patted her hair down like it was neat and tidy. "The gun had been hidden away, out of his reach, but this one day, I walked into the back room and Pa was cradling it, looking at it like he was waiting for it to say something. 'Don't tell your ma,' he says to me. 'I'm going hunting tomorrow and I'm going to surprise her with rabbit.' I believed him. I actually thought it was an answered prayer, that he was getting back to his old self."

The boy saw the trail now, the path where this story was leading. And it made him sit up.

"That night while we were sleeping, he went down by the henhouse and finished it." Ruth shut her eyes and put a hand to her mouth. Samuel saw that her fingers were trembling. "I never told anyone about the gun, but I knew Ma blamed me for not keeping him from himself. She hated Pa for what he did and she hated me just as well.

Gave me such a beating. I took it, too. Know why, Samuel?" A great moan rushed up and out of her. "I was glad for Pa, God help me. He had his peace and I was glad."

Ruth sniffed hard and pulled herself up, her heavy eyes finding Samuel. "My pa was haunted by his thoughts and I can see the same thing happening with you. It's got to stop. I know you're a boy, and seldom does a sensible thought enter a boy's head, but you must rid your mind of these malicious thoughts. It's a poison, and unless you fight against it, Samuel, the venom will destroy you and me both. I'm an honest woman with a good reputation and I won't have you spreading this nonsense any further, do you hear?"

Samuel couldn't look at her. But he nodded.

"I've been working in this house since you were two, and though it's not my way to show it, I've always had the softest spot of all for you. That's right, don't look so shocked. Which is why it upsets me so, to think you really believe I could do something so unspeakable." She stood up quickly, then needed the wall to steady herself. "Well, this foolishness stops here and now. Are you very clear on that, Samuel Clay?"

"Yes."

"I'll need the lamp to see myself out." Ruth turned and made for the door. "Shut it off when I'm gone and good night to you."

When the bedroom was once again in darkness, Samuel put his hand to his chest and felt it beating. And though he could feel the fear, he sensed that something else was causing it to thump so wildly—the excitement of a hunter catching its prey. Ruth thought she'd been setting his mind to rest with her story, but she had unwittingly given the game away. She was happy her father was dead; she said it made her glad. If Samuel had needed any further proof that Ruth was a killer, he had it now.

28

For all her sins, it was a length of red yarn that would be her undoing. Samuel couldn't help but smile about that. It was the reason he was down in his mother's study switching on a lamp in the dead of night. This breakthrough began with the postcards. No, it began when he couldn't sleep, so full of thoughts about Ruth wanting her father dead and how this testimony of her black heart, coming right from her very own lips, was a greater burden than the boy had imagined. For it confirmed something unspeakable about his mother. But while it was proof enough for him, he couldn't pretend it was evidence. Wouldn't it still be her word against his? And didn't Ruth have a way with words and could twist just about anything to her own ends?

He needed her diary. Or something else that would prove her guilt. Surely if he thought on it long enough something would materialize. The whole thing seemed to take hours and yielded nothing of any use, which Samuel had taken as a personal failing. Picking up the postcards from the side table was more a reflex than anything. He'd read each one a thousand times, but their magic, he reasoned, the warmth that blossomed in his belly when he held one, must be absent now that he knew they were probably written by Ruth's wicked accomplice in America. Still, the handwriting was so like his mother's, the words, too, that he couldn't pretend they didn't make him feel close to her.

The pictures on the back of each card—a harbor, a bridge, a skyline—were as familiar to Samuel as the writing itself. As he gazed at them, or through them, his mind flew to the atlas and the tiny green flags and the red yarn he had tethered to each pin and the tugboat, trailing the yarn and stranded out in the Atlantic. What a stupid exercise that had been. He'd been captured by Ruth's lie that his mother was sailing home. Hadn't he eaten up every rotten word? Samuel had sighed then, thinking on the atlas and how his hopes and dreams about his mother were fixed in its pages just as surely as each pin and tag.

It came to him without warning and without effort, as the right thought will sometimes do. With the postcards in his hand and the map in his mind's eye, an idea simply dropped into his head, fully formed. A thought so full of possibility it made him gasp. Was it the fly in the ointment of Ruth's murderous scheme? Samuel looked down at the postcards, finding the one he needed. He read it over. Then he practically leaped from the bed, the cards in hand, and crept down to his mother's study as quietly as he could.

A pool of dim light washed half-heartedly from

the lamp, barely reaching the atlas. But it was enough. Samuel's eyes traveled along the tracks of red yarn—San Francisco, Dallas, Los Angeles, Florida, Pennsylvania, Toronto, New York City, Boston. But it was the West Coast that drew him back. He lifted the postcard sent from Dallas, Texas, and dated May 24.

> Dearest Samuel,
> Are you missing me as dreadfully as I miss you? San Francisco wasn't the great success I hoped it would be—bankers lack imagination by nature, but honestly, what an insipid lot. Their loss! I've roared into Dallas without a backward glance, determined to win friends and open checkbooks. I'll be home as soon as I can manage, my little man. Be good for Ruth.
>
> With love and kisses,
> Mother

Though he had read that postcard too many times to count, just like all the others, this time the words seemed to fracture under his watchful gaze, cracking open, to reveal the dark heart underneath the ornate handwriting. His mother wrote of arriving in Dallas after her disappointment in San Francisco *without a backward glance*—that's what she said. Yet in the very next postcard, sent ten days later, she was in Los Angeles. That postcard was mainly about the weather, which was oppressively hot, and a promise that she would write again once she reached Florida. So his mother had gone back to California despite leaving the West Coast with no intention of returning there.

Samuel set down the postcard, returning his attention to the atlas. He ran his finger along the yarn from Dallas to Los Angeles. His mother had gone back when the postcard made clear that she was only moving forward. It didn't make sense. Ruth had made a mistake, that much he knew. But the implications were dizzying and raised other possibilities, which, given the late hour and the ghoulish thrill of this new discovery, the boy could hardly be expected to resist. What if the contrary postcard was a signal from his mother that she was trapped? Locked up somewhere in America by Ruth's vile accomplice? It was a thought. His mother was being forced to write the postcards against her will and, being a clever sort, had planted a code, something only Samuel could decode. A cipher that would let him know something was wrong. Was that likely? Samuel didn't pretend the whole thing wasn't confounding, but weren't most foul plots complex by design?

The facts didn't lie. In the postcard from Dallas

his mother wrote of having left San Francisco (and therefore California) without a backward glance and then in the next breath she had returned there. Why would she do such a thing? Her words contradicted her actions, and if she had gone back, why not explain the reason in her next postcard? Instead, she had just prattled on about the weather. The boy was looking at the card now, shaking his head. It was shameful that it had taken him so long to see it, and though he wasn't completely sure what it all proved—a conspiracy this wicked was bound to be unfathomable to someone without a criminal mind—he only knew that he had found a fault line in the fiction that his mother was merrily traveling across America, trying to save the family steel mill. And that meant something else, too. Ruth wasn't nearly as smart as she thought she was.

The park was crowded like every other Saturday so the ducks were spoiled for choice. But Samuel wasn't really paying attention. He stood on the edge of the pond, next to a mother with her two young children, both boys. The woman was crouched down talking to the little ones about this duck or that—she even had names for them—and all the while she had a hand in the small of each boy's back. There was such tenderness about this, and Samuel didn't want to hate the boys for it, but it was a struggle.

Ruth had done well at the market that morning. All the shortbread had sold and most of the tea cakes. As they were packing up, Mrs. Pryce, the reverend's wife, came over to ask Ruth if she could fill a large order of tea cakes and lemon tarts for Monday, as she had the church committee coming for morning tea and her cook had broken her wrist and was utterly useless. That was why Samuel was standing alone by the pond. Ruth was still chatting with Mrs. Pryce, pretending as if she were the nicest housekeeper there ever was.

The boy hadn't slept after returning to his bedroom. Well, not very much. How could he? There was his new discovery about the postcards to reckon with, not to mention Ruth practically confessing her wickedness about being happy her father had killed himself. Didn't she just about put the gun in his hand? So it was not a great stretch to think she had done something equally rotten to his mother. The theory that she was being held captive in America had lost some of its power in the hard light of day. Was it really likely? No, he doubted his mother ever set sail for America. Whatever had happened to her, Ruth was behind it. The atlas pointed the way, if you only cared to look. But who could he convince to see things as clearly as he did?

"Waste of good bread." Ruth came up behind him buttoning up her brown coat. "The ducks are too well-fed to pay you any mind."

She'd been back to her old self by morning, her hair pulled back, her face set in a faint scowl, barely saying two words to him at breakfast. Samuel figured she was probably angry with herself for revealing just what a monster she was last night. He didn't know why Ruth had talked so freely, so differently from how she spoke during the day—perhaps she was sleepy and sleepy people forget themselves and say things they otherwise wouldn't. Perhaps that was it.

The mother with the two small boys gave Samuel a smile and he did his best to return it. "I don't mind when they're not hungry," she told him. "In winter they must be starving so I suppose they save it all up until then."

"Greedy is more like it," Ruth said. She had no tolerance for gluttony, even in ducks. "If they didn't grab at every little thing, they wouldn't fill up so fast."

The mother stood up then and took each of her children by the hand, leading them off with promises of toffee apples at the market. The boys squealed as if she had promised them a year of Christmases and Samuel's eyes followed them as they walked off.

"Spoiled rotten, I should think," muttered Ruth. "Come on, it's time we were going. You have the psalm to finish and I have six dozen lemon tarts and four strawberry tea cakes to make."

They headed home and Ruth got started on

her baking, while Samuel was instructed to sit at the kitchen table and get to work on his Bible passage. As Ruth rushed about, she would mumble to herself or hum what to Samuel sounded like funeral music. He stayed quiet, looking down at the great book but not doing very much of anything.

Proof, that's what he needed. Ruth was a crafty sort and she must have hidden his mother someplace no one would find her. She wasn't in the cellar or the woodshed or the stables. She wasn't anywhere. Which meant Samuel needed Ruth's diary. Of course, he didn't know for certain that Ruth even had a diary but what else could she have been writing in the dead of night? And when she heard Samuel at the door, hadn't she hidden it away in the drawer as if she were terrified he might see it? Yes, there had to be a diary—that's what he needed to prove what Ruth had done. That's what he needed so that she should be strung up by the neck until she was dead.

Samuel stood.

"Where do you think you're going?" Ruth was cracking eggs into a bowl.

"I need pencils to draw the picture for Reverend Pryce," he told her. "They're upstairs in my bed-room."

Ruth sniffed. "Be quick about it."

The boy took the back stairs and ran the whole way.

"No need to pound those stairs!" Ruth yelled from below. "I have enough of a headache without your assistance, Samuel Clay."

"Sorry, Ruth!"

Samuel hardly slowed as he moved across the landing. His thinking was very simple. The faster he moved, the more time he would have upstairs to find Ruth's diary. She'd probably written down all the nasty details. What she had done to his mother and how she had suffered and called out for Samuel. And Ruth would certainly have written down where his mother was lying, all alone in some horrid dark hole. Did she know how hard he was trying to find her? Did his mother see him and love him even more for what he was doing?

He thought she must. That she was looking down right at that very moment.

Samuel didn't pause at Ruth's bedroom door and say a prayer to his father that it would be unlocked. He just grabbed the doorknob and pushed. But it didn't yield. He tried again in the way that a boy does when he hopes that the second time the door won't be as locked as it was the first time. But, of course, it always is. Ruth's door had never been locked before, as far as he could recall. It's not that she ever invited him in, but she'd never forbidden it, either. And if he'd ever needed to ask her this or that and she was in her bedroom, he would knock and she would say,

"Come in," and the door would be unlocked. But not now.

Only a person with something terrible to hide would lock her bedroom door. Something about having his worst fears confirmed hit Samuel like a slap to the face. It wasn't a poison eating up his mind, like Ruth had said. A locked door was real enough. And hadn't Ruth been happy her father took a gun down by the henhouse and shot himself? That was real enough. And Ruth stealing his mother's jewelry? Real enough.

Samuel wasn't aware he was crying. Not at first, because he was angry and anger usually blew away the sorrow or at least made it harder to find. Then he heard his own shaky breaths and the broken sobs, which were made even more wretched in the silence of the corridor. She wasn't coming back. Ruth had truly killed her and she wasn't ever coming home. He remembered the dream he had had—his mother breezing into the hall, sunlight pouring around her, and the smile on her face that promised brighter days. He'd been right. It would never happen.

The boy ran then, toward her bedroom door. He tried to open it, but thanks to Ruth, this small part of his mother had been taken from him, too. His legs had a mind of their own, and as Samuel wiped his eyes, he saw through a fog of tears that he was running down the corridor to the very last door. His mother's dressing room. He'd been in there a few times since she disappeared, but Samuel was always mindful that his mother didn't welcome him there.

He opened the door and stepped inside. Sniffing and wiping his nose, the boy looked around. The dressing room was large and abounding in sunlight. Along three walls were a collection of oak wardrobes, and across the fourth was a row of windows and, in between, three mirrors all at different angles so his mother could catch herself from every side. In the middle of the room was a round red velvet lounge and beside it stood a mannequin that his mother liked to hang her very best dresses on for reasons Samuel couldn't fathom. The mannequin was bare, its limbless form the very shape and size of his mother. So it made sense, then, that Samuel would wrap his arms around it and tuck his head under its bust. He knew it was wrong—his mother had caught him doing that once before and had been very cross—but right now he hoped she would understand.

When he had stopped crying and let go, Samuel walked slowly around the dressing room. He opened some of the wardrobes, looking inside; most of his mother's dresses were gone and the few that hung there looked rather lonely. Ruth must have taken the clothes away so that it would look like his mother had packed them all into trunks for her voyage to America. She was a cunning one, old Ruth.

The largest of the wardrobes took up almost half a wall, its bronzed panels arranged into a diamond pattern. Samuel opened the heavy door and saw a single dress hanging there. Still, it caused his stomach to tingle and flutter. For it was a red dress made of silk, with a large pleated skirt that looked like the surface of a windswept pond.

The memory bloomed inside of him and it felt as if he were falling. The room suddenly darkened and the wardrobe melted away as if made of mud, leaving only the dress. It was moving now, drifting across the room, and as it did it began to take shape and fill out—and then she was there in front of him, fixing her hair in the mirror.

"Mother." The word practically flew out of him. "Mother, I'm here."

The light seemed to dance around her, hitting her pale shoulders and bouncing off. She touched her earrings, the ones his father had given her on their wedding day, and looked around, smiling. She said something, Samuel couldn't hear what, and then his father walked over, dressed in tails and a bow tie, kissing her cheek.

"Mother," said Samuel, "it's me. I'm here."

They were going out, he knew that. Going somewhere very important, and knowing that filled him with a dread so fierce he had to shut his eyes tight and swallow the shout that wanted to come up. When he opened them again he could see himself, younger than he was now. He was flying across the dressing room, rushing at her. When he reached his mother he threw his arms around her waist.

"Not now, darling." He could hear the sweet music of her voice. She slipped her hands behind her back and unspooled his fingers. "Mummy's running late. Ruth!"

"He just wants to say good night," said his father.

The boy was crying. He put his arms around his mother again and buried his head in her stomach. "He's already said good night," said the beautiful creature. "It's ridiculous that he does this every time we leave the house." Then, "Ruth? Where can she be?"

"Don't go," the boy was saying, "it's a stupid party. Please don't go."

His mother pulled his hands from around her again. "I can't, darling, I can't."

Samuel thought she was talking to him but then his father came over and gently moved the boy away. But it wouldn't do. The boy yanked free and ran back to her. There were no words to explain it; he just had to find a way to keep her in place, to fix her to the ground so that she would stay. So that she would stop going away.

"When will you be home?" The boy was holding his mother's hand but it kept slipping from his grasp. "When will you come home? I will wait up for you."

His mother didn't say anything; she just shook her head crossly and turned away. "Ruth, you're needed up here!"

The boy was young and stupid back then— he didn't understand what was clear enough to Samuel now. These parties were important because a great many important people were there and they might be able to help with the steel mill. And there was so little time to set things right, his mother didn't have time to play cards with him or hide-and-seek or take him to the park to feed the ducks. Ruth was better at that kind of thing, and besides, it would bore him to always be by her side, and truly, if she was always unthreading his arms or pulling away, it had nothing to do with Samuel. He was her little man, everyone knew that, but he had to know that being a grown-up was a complicated matter, and as his father told him over and over, his mother was doing the very best she could.

"Ruth," called his mother again, "where are you?"

The bedroom door shut with great force. None of the windows were open in the dressing room but the door behind Samuel closed with an unholy bang. Just like that the dressing room emptied—his mother and father and his younger self crumbled to dust, swept away as if on the same strong wind that had blown the door. The boy had jumped rather pitifully and spun around. Doors that close themselves are troubling things. So Samuel rushed at it and threw it open. That was the plan, anyway. But the door would not yield. He twisted the handle and pulled hard, but the door refused to budge.

He heard his mother's laugh then. But not her normal laugh, musical and light; this seemed to scratch its way across the empty room like a scornful snicker. Samuel looked back. The room was utterly still and silent, save for the odd snap and creek of its old bones. Only the mannequin, in the very shape and form of his mother, loomed over the chamber. It was probably a trick of the light, how it now seemed to be regarding him with great interest.

"Don't go." They were his words but the voice belonged to her. "Please don't go."

She was mocking him.

"Mother?" Samuel moved away, feeling the door at his back.

"When will you come home?" His mother was laughing again. "I will wait up for you."

"Stop," Samuel whispered.

It wasn't her. It couldn't be. She loved him best of all.

"Mother, it's me," she hissed. "I'm here."

"Stop!" The boy was pounding the door now. "Go away!"

The door swung open, pushing him back. He stumbled and fell to the floor and Ruth was looking down at him, frowning. "What on earth?"

Samuel got to his feet and looked behind him. The mannequin seemed rooted to the floor once again, lifeless and not the least bit menacing.

"I suppose you'd have me believe you were looking for your pencils in here, then?" said Ruth. "Why were you making such a racket?"

"The door was locked." He turned back to regard the housekeeper. "Did you lock it?"

"What a thing to ask."

"I couldn't open the door."

"Perhaps it was stuck."

The boy said, "It wasn't stuck."

"Who were you talking to?" Ruth's voice was tight.

"You heard her?" he asked.

"What?" Ruth entered the room and walked around it with a scowl, opening and closing cupboards. "Heard who? Who were you talking to? And this time I want the truth."

Samuel pointed silently to the open wardrobe and the silk dress hanging there.

Ruth looked in at the gown and then down at the boy, her eyes drifting about his face. "What fresh nonsense is this, Samuel?"

It was as if the boy couldn't hear her.

"Samuel, who were you talking to?"

When no answer was given, the uncertainty in

Ruth's voice was washed away, replaced by the safer waters of her censure.

"You know the rules—this room is out of bounds. I've had all I can take of you wandering where you don't belong. Must I barricade every room in this blessed house?"

The boy gazed only at the dress, for that was the best of her. His mother would never make fun of him; her laugh would never be cruel. Ruth looked at the red dress, too, a good deal longer than she might have liked, and then she said, "Utter nonsense," shutting the wardrobe with some force.

29

It was all her fault. The whole reason Samuel was bent forward, climbing up the hill in the heat of the afternoon with a pound of flour in his hand. It was because of her. Ruth had to make six dozen lemon tarts and four tea cakes—wouldn't she know how much flour she was going to need before she got started? No, due to the fact that she spent half her time chasing after Samuel, she had miscalculated. So now he'd been sent into the village to fetch a pound. Ruth had instructed him to run the whole way, as if she were sending him on a mission to save England. He hated her.

The whole walk, there and back, had been spent wondering about how to get hold of the diary. The postcards and atlas were powerful weapons but he needed more. And in order to reach the diary, Samuel knew he had to get hold of the key to her bedroom. He didn't know for certain, but he guessed that Ruth might have it in the pocket of her apron. Hadn't he seen her put the key to his mother's bedroom in there? But getting hold of it wouldn't be easy. Perhaps he could spill something on Ruth, something sure to leave a stain like hot chocolate or strawberry jelly, and then she'd need to take it off and he could offer to carry it to the laundry for her? No, that wouldn't work. Ruth was wicked but she wasn't stupid. There had to be another way in; he just didn't know what.

Samuel was still panting as he came up the drive, feeling hot and puffed and, as such, entirely justified in stopping off to see Robin Hood in the kitchen garden. But the rabbit was nowhere to be found. The boy's mood was now grimmer than ever, as he came around the front of the house, kicking the gravel and cursing Ruth. So at first he didn't notice the car parked under the portico. When he did, he hadn't a clue whom it belonged to. It was a glossy red with a fold-down top and white leather seats.

As soon as the front door opened, the echo of voices carried out into the great hall. He heard Ruth's hideous laugh, which sounded just like a cackle, and another besides. It was deep and rich, and because he had heard it before, the boy started to run toward the kitchen.

"None of that galloping about, thank you," Ruth said as he plunged through the door. As admonishments went, this one sounded positively jovial.

"Sammy!" His uncle stood up and shook his hand like they were old chums. "Been down to the shops, have you, ducky? Ruth working you hard, is she?"

Samuel found that he couldn't stop looking at

his uncle Felix—as if he didn't quite believe that he was there. "Yes."

"Don't believe a word of it." Ruth's voice bubbled to life. "He's the one running me off my feet."

His uncle tapped him playfully on the cheek. "That right, Sammy?"

The boy shrugged. "I thought you were going to London?"

"I'm on my way, as it happens. A few things came up that needed my attention and I thought, wouldn't it be just the thing, to call in and see Sammy before I go?"

Samuel wanted to hug his uncle but thought it might seem unexpected.

"I've been telling your uncle how well you're doing at school." Ruth had set her baking trays to one side and was sitting in front of a pot of tea and two cups.

"I was useless at school." Samuel's uncle sat down and crossed his legs. "Your father was the one with all the brains, Sammy." He threw a crooked grin at Ruth. "Mind if I smoke?"

Ruth said she didn't mind at all. Samuel watched as his uncle took out a silver cigarette case and matching lighter and lit up, the smoke coiling from the end of the cigarette like a serpent. His uncle had come to see him. He must have understood that something terrible had happened and now he was here to help him.

"Would you like another shortbread, Mr. Clay?" Ruth pushed the plate toward him.

"Don't mind if I do."

Only one thing stood in Samuel's way.

"Mother's been sending me postcards," Samuel said, setting the flour down on the counter. "Would you like to see?"

"I'm sure your uncle wouldn't be interested in those postcards," Ruth said.

"Oh, I don't know about that." His uncle took a drag on his cigarette, throwing his head back and blowing the smoke up toward the ceiling. He winked at Samuel. "Show me."

"They're up in my bedroom." Samuel said this pointing toward the door. "If you'd like to come up, I'll show you my planes, as well."

"Mr. Clay is only here for a short time," said Ruth, pouring the tea. "If you must show him the cards, you go up and get them. I'm sure your uncle doesn't want to be climbing up and down the stairs all afternoon."

With a heavy heart, Samuel went and fetched the postcards. Ruth wasn't going to leave him alone with his uncle. Not without a fight. Luckily, a new plan hatched while he was walking down the back stairs.

As his uncle looked over the postcards, finally selecting the one from Dallas, Samuel watched him carefully. Looking for any sign, the faintest flicker in his eyes, any recognition that something about this whole thing wasn't right.

Then he put the last postcard down and said, "Your mother's in Boston now?"

Samuel nodded. He wanted desperately to say something else but didn't dare.

"Mrs. Clay has been all over America, it seems, meeting with the bankers and such," said Ruth. "Samuel would love to hear from her more frequently, but as I've tried to explain to him, time runs away on you when you're abroad."

"Well, yes, I suppose it does," said his uncle.

"I have an atlas," declared Samuel. "Father bought it for Mother, but now it's mine, I suppose. I have pins showing where mother has been and yarn connecting all the places . . . and I could show you if you like?"

"Samuel . . ." Ruth started to say.

"I'd bring it in here but it's very big and the pins might fall out." Samuel spoke rapidly, not wanting to let Ruth interrupt. "Won't you come and see it, Uncle Felix?"

His uncle stubbed out his cigarette. "Lead the way, ducky."

Ruth stood up at the same time as Samuel's uncle. But the boy had already thought of that.

"Ruth, you should go on with your baking." He turned to his uncle, snatching up the postcards. "Ruth has a big order and they have to be ready by Monday. We need the money, you see."

This caused his uncle to laugh and put a hand

on Samuel's shoulder. But Ruth was beaten and she knew it. "Mind you don't keep your uncle long," she said. "He has a train to catch."

As they walked to the study, there was a lot of talk about his uncle's travels—it seemed he had been everywhere, including Boston. Samuel never could work out what his uncle did for a living but his mother once said that all Felix did well was spend money. Part of the reason Samuel was sent to the local school and not somewhere more distinguished, like his father and uncle had, was because his mother didn't want him turning out like his uncle Felix, who she said was a pompous buffoon wrapped in tweed, dipped in gin and rolled in horsehair. She said it was a miracle Samuel's father had been so well-adjusted and not even slightly an ass.

"Do you like it?" said Samuel.

His uncle was crouched down, gazing at the atlas and all the pins, which looked like tiny flags. When he pushed the tugboat toward England, the yarn stretching out behind it like a scarlet current, Samuel couldn't help but feel a certain amount of pride. "Damn fine job, Sammy." Uncle Felix looked at his nephew. "Must help, seeing that she isn't so very far away."

No, it didn't help at all. Samuel looked to the door to make sure Ruth wasn't there. "You noticed, didn't you, Uncle Felix, about the postcards?"

"Noticed? Of course, ducky. They're terrific. You've got quite a collection."

"No." Samuel pushed the postcard from Dallas at his uncle. "Mother didn't plan on going back to California. She says so right there—'without a backward glance.' But in the next postcard . . ." Now the boy pushed that one into Uncle Felix's hand. "See? It's from Los Angeles. She went back even though she said she wouldn't." Samuel pointed at the atlas. "Look, you can see that Mother left the West Coast and was moving east, then all of a sudden she turned back. Why would she do that?"

Uncle Felix read over both postcards carefully and spent some time looking at the atlas, following the path of pins and yarn. His uncle gave every indication of taking the boy seriously and Samuel felt a lump swelling in his throat that without urgent intervention would give rise to a loud and undignified sob. When Uncle Felix was done, he clicked his tongue as if to indicate a degree of bafflement that could only help the boy's cause.

"You have a point, ducky," Uncle Felix said, "but I'm not sure it proves anything."

" 'Without a backward glance,' that's what she said." Samuel spoke with complete authority. "So why turn around and head back to California?"

"Well, let's see." As a general rule, Uncle Felix was wary of serious contemplation, so it was not altogether surprising when his frown smoothed out in mere seconds. He even slapped his knee. "Doesn't your mother have an aunt who lives in Los Angeles?"

Samuel didn't know.

Uncle Felix was nodding now. "I think your parents visited her on their honeymoon. Yes, that's it. I recall something about a rather enchanting estate high up in the hills. If memory serves, the old girl's a dried-up spinster with more money than Augustus Caesar."

"So?" said Samuel, and the word was delivered with unvarnished contempt.

"Well, we all know your grandfather is a tight-fisted humbug, so perhaps your mother wanted to rattle another branch of the family tree, hoping to loosen a few banknotes? She'd be a fool not to try, seems to me." His smile was horribly self-satisfied. "So you see, Sammy, no great mystery."

"Mother wouldn't do it, Uncle Felix." Samuel stole another look at the door and spoke in a whisper. "She wouldn't go so far away and for so long. I think . . ."

His uncle's smile wasn't unkind. "You think what, Sammy?"

Samuel bent his head. "I think Ruth knows where she is."

"Ruth?"

Samuel nodded.

"Well, of course she does. Ruth's the one who first told me your mother had taken off for America."

"No." Samuel looked at the door again. "I think she did something."

"To your mother?"

Samuel nodded.

"Come and sit with me." His uncle pulled up a chair and had Samuel sit down on his knee, which made the boy feel like a toddler. "Now, Ruth told me you haven't been yourself lately and that you miss your mother very much and it's making you . . . it's upsetting you. Which is perfectly natural, Sammy, don't you think it isn't. Look here, I'm the first person to think badly of someone—I have a gift for it, you could say— but this thing about Ruth, I don't think it's very likely. Why would she do anything unpleasant to your mother?"

"She was going to lose her job. Mother was going to get rid of her."

"Of Ruth? I find that hard to believe. Your mother used to say Ruth was the only thing keeping her sane in this madhouse. And what about the postcards? You must see that your mother wrote those and how could she be sending you cards from America if Ruth had done something unspeakable to her?"

Samuel didn't have an answer for that.

"Ruth is a stern sort, her kind usually are.

Gives you a smack when you're cheeky, does she?"

The boy stayed quiet.

"Your father and I were always getting walloped by our nanny. Little terrors we were."

Samuel's eyes drifted to the atlas. "Ruth tells lies."

"I'm sure she does. I'm willing to bet that you tell the odd porky yourself. We all do, ducky, it's hardly a hanging offense."

"She took Mother's best jewels." Samuel was fixed on his uncle now, staring intently, so that not a single word could fall away or be misunderstood. "She stole them, Uncle Felix. I caught her red-handed. Please, you have to believe me."

"Of course I believe you, Sammy." Uncle Felix patted the boy's back and his tone was tender and patronizing all at once. "Life's a complicated thing, ducky, difficult and untidy. You'll understand that when you're a bit older. Ruth told me about the jewels, and as hard as it might be to understand, she didn't take them for personal gain. It's her job to keep the house running and make sure you have everything you need—and that takes money. Rather a lot of it, in fact." He patted Samuel's back again. "Don't you think it's a tad unfair, calling Ruth a thief, when she was only doing as your mother asked?"

Just like that, the bright hope of this unexpected visitor, that surge of joy that had lit Samuel up like a lantern, was snuffed out. Ruth had got to him first.

"Something has happened to my mother, I know it has."

"Are you sleeping, Sammy?" said the uncle. "You look awfully tired."

"Ruth took her away from me."

Uncle Felix exhaled like he was smoking a cigarette. "These fears about your mother aren't good for you, not one little bit. Don't you think I'd call the police if I thought there was any truth to it? You're my favorite nephew—you're my only nephew, but that's by the by—so I wouldn't steer you wrong, would I? Tell you what—I'm so sure your mother's in America, I'll wager you five pounds. How's that?"

"When you get to London would you check, Uncle Felix?"

"Check what?"

"Check if Mother took a boat to America. There must be a way to check."

"Well, yes, I suppose there is."

"Will you do it? Will you check?"

His uncle thought on this for only a moment. "It's a promise. I'll do it first thing, you have my word."

"And you won't say anything about this to Ruth?"

"Don't look so alarmed, Sammy, it's not as bad as all that."

"You won't tell her what I told you. Promise you won't tell."

"Not a word, Sammy, not one word."

But he was looking at the boy like he wasn't at all well, and Samuel didn't believe him.

30

They never took meals in the dining room but Ruth had made an exception. The kitchen table, where they usually ate, was crowded with trays and racks full of tea cakes and lemon tarts. The whole house smelled heavenly, though Samuel wasn't allowed to taste so much as a crumb. The reverend's wife was paying good money and there were none to spare. Besides, Ruth said they needed time to cool—which is why they were eating dinner elsewhere.

"It was very good of your uncle to come and see you, wasn't it?" Ruth set the plate of roasted meat down on the table with some care. "Samuel?"

The boy looked up.

"I said, wasn't it good of your uncle to come and see you?"

"Yes," Samuel said.

Ruth picked up a serving fork and the large carving knife and got to work on the roast. It was impossible for Samuel not to stare at the blade.

"Did you two have a good talk, then?" Ruth said.

"I showed him the atlas."

"And was he impressed?"

Samuel shrugged. "He liked it."

"You were in the study a very long time." The smooth back and forth of the blade, as it sliced through the animal, was suddenly arrested as Ruth hit a bone. Samuel watched her face lock up, and then the whites of her knuckles as she pushed the knife down, snapping the bone in two. "I would imagine you were talking about more than the atlas?"

Samuel shrugged again.

Which is when Ruth stopped carving. "Or is it a great secret, what you were talking about?"

"It's not a secret." Samuel cast about for something he could use. "Uncle Felix was telling me about when he and Father were boys and all the naughty things they did." Samuel forced a smile. "It was funny."

"I'm sure it was." Ruth picked up a piece of meat and put it on the boy's plate. "Your uncle is entertaining, that's for certain. Your father always said he would make a fine writer, if only he'd settle down and apply himself."

They sat at one end of the long table with an oil lamp between them. Ruth said the chandelier was too costly to turn on for just the two of them. She then muttered something about the fine dinner parties that had been held there and she said this so wistfully that Samuel was left in little doubt that those days were splendid and far behind them. For his part, the boy would have preferred the bright light of the chandelier, as the oil lamp could hardly compete with the dark red walls, and its soft glow had such a faint reach it felt as if he and Ruth were trapped in a flickering bubble.

Ruth took her seat at the head of the table. "I did ask him to stay for dinner—he's always spoken highly of my roast rabbit—but he seemed in a mad rush to get down to London."

He is going there to prove that Mother never did sail for America. That's what Samuel wanted to say but, of course, he didn't. Not just because Ruth had forbidden any such talk but also because Samuel doubted his uncle Felix would even look into it. Yes, he had promised, given his word, but he also promised to have Samuel over to stay during the summer and he never did. And Ruth had gotten in his ear and filled it with lies about the boy's sickly mind. It wasn't his poor mother Uncle Felix was worried about; it was Samuel. Everything was so wrong and unjust that Samuel didn't care for any of Ruth's roast rabbit or her chestnut stuffing.

"I don't know where your appetite has gone." Ruth was sprinkling salt over Samuel's potatoes even though he never asked her to. "You're already much too thin, just like your mother. People will think I'm not feeding you."

"I'm not hungry."

"Nonsense. What boy of nine isn't on the brink of starvation most of the time?" Ruth filled her plate, arranging the vegetables with some care.

"You forget that I've cooked for you most of your life, Samuel Clay, and I know your stomach is a bottomless pit."

Samuel watched the heat rise up from his plate and he blew on it. The steam wafted over the table with such promise but in mere seconds it vanished as if it had never been there to begin with.

"It's bad enough . . ." Ruth appeared to think better of it and ended the sentence there. She pierced a potato with her fork and sliced it cleanly down the middle. An impressive cloud billowed up from its parted flesh, and as Samuel watched—how could he not?—Ruth smiled faintly and blew on it, sending puffs of steam over her plate. Ruth saw the look of surprise in the boy's eyes and it must have pleased her. "I was a child once myself, you know." She motioned to his plate. "Mind it doesn't get cold. I made this perfectly lovely meal just for you, Samuel."

The boy sighed heavily and stabbed a piece of meat with his fork. He didn't want to eat, didn't want to please Ruth in any way, but it was as if his hands, his very fingers, moved under Ruth's command and he had nothing to say about it. The meat took some chewing, the texture tough and unyielding, and Samuel's face buckled into a grimace as he swallowed it down.

"Gravy?" When Samuel shook his head rather

crossly, Ruth huffed. "There was a time when you'd devour my roast rabbit with chestnut stuffing and be on to a second helping before I'd even sat down. What will your mother say when she comes home and finds you a shadow of the boy she left behind?"

The mention of his mother made Samuel want to fly at her, knocking her to the ground. But he didn't, because now his whole self was fixed on the roast as if he were seeing it, really seeing it, for the first time. He said, "Rabbit."

Ruth nodded and took her first bite. "It's not exactly tender, but the flavor's good, if I do say so myself."

The boy looked only at the roasted animal. "You said the butcher wouldn't sell you a rabbit until you've paid the bill."

Ruth sniffed. "Eat up while it's hot."

Samuel shifted his gaze to Ruth. "Did you pay the bill, Ruth?"

"Enough chatter, young man. Eat your dinner."

"Ruth?"

She met his stare then, her dark eyes sparking like struck flint in the lamplight. "I suppose you'd have been happy with a boiled turnip for supper?"

The chair was still tumbling over as Samuel reached the doorway. He ran through the hall and into the kitchen, finding himself tearing around the room, every conceivable surface covered in lemon tarts and tea cakes. This was an unexpected comfort. Ruth bought all her meat skinned or plucked because she had enough to do as it was. There was no sign of the sort of ghoulish work that might have involved Robin Hood. The knot in his stomach was starting to slacken, and his mind was turning to how he might explain himself to Ruth. That's when he glanced down into the sink and saw the knife. It was smeared in blood, which ran across the blade and pooled around the edges like a crimson shadow.

Running outside wasn't a choice, he just found himself there. Perhaps it was to prove that Robin Hood was under his favorite hedge, staring longingly at the row of cabbages. But Samuel never made it past the back door. For on the stone steps was a bucket and even in the pale moonlight the boy could see its contents—the puddle of entrails and blood and the folds of the muddy-brown coat with that hint of ginger. He didn't gasp or cry out or even cover his mouth. But the finality of this discovery felt like two hands pushing down on his shoulders. He was certain she had left these remains there so that he might find them.

Returning to the dining room was the only thing left to do. He walked into the darkened chamber with some purpose and marched over to the table, standing beside Ruth as if his mere presence would be censure enough to make her crumble. But it wasn't.

"Finished?" she said as if he had been having a frivolous tantrum.

"I know what you did," said the boy.

"And what is that?"

"Why?" That's what he said next and it was an honest question seeking an answer. "Why, Ruth?"

"We have to eat, don't we?" She sniffed. "Sit down and finish your supper."

"I won't take another bite!" This was shouted without restraint.

"Suit yourself." Ruth didn't look up from her plate. "Wash up and take yourself to bed, then."

And despite everything, the boy did as he was told.

"Did you brush your teeth?"

Silence.

"Samuel, I asked you a question."

It was his only weapon and he used it boldly, turning his head away.

"Samuel, I'm in no mood for this." Her voice was stony. "Did you brush your teeth?"

The boy sighed. "Yes."

"Yes, what?"

"Yes, Ruth."

"Are you sure about that?"

Samuel nodded.

She pulled the covers up under Samuel's arms despite his attempts to resist and made a few comments about the state of his bedroom and the fact that tomorrow it would need a thorough cleaning and he was going to help because she had to finish decorating the tea cakes and lemon tarts and the sitting room windows were in a state and would need seeing to and did Samuel realize how this big house could just about break your spirit with its endless demands?

When Samuel made no reply, his eyes fixed on the window, Ruth took a long breath. "You're not the first child to lose an animal to the dinner table. I had pets when I was your age, all kinds— the farm was teeming with hares and chickens and pigs. I stopped naming them after a while because I knew that my pa wouldn't spare them. It's unfortunate, but that's just the way it is. And around here, with an empty purse and a pile of unpaid bills, rabbits aren't pets, Samuel, they're food. It's my job to keep you healthy and strong and I won't apologize for putting a wholesome meal on your plate."

Ruth was a monster whose cruel heart swelled with gladness at every suffering. She killed things, things you cared for and named and perhaps even loved, cutting throats and stripping the fur from flesh. She did it with glee and served it up as a kind of torment, knowing that you would gobble up the thing you love, chew it up and swallow it down, and then have to live with the shame of doing so. Samuel looked up at this foul creature.

"I hate you."

This caused Ruth to sniff and pick up the clock beside his bed, wiping underneath with the hem of her apron. "Well, that's your right."

Samuel held his fingers up to the lamp and watched the light collect around them. If he appeared to be playing now, he wasn't. All the while his mind, which wasn't even a tiny bit unwell, spun with ideas about getting his hands on Ruth's diary. That was the only way to make her pay. But he had to get the key to her bedroom first—or else find some other way in.

"Regardless of your feelings for me, don't think I've forgotten about your schoolwork." Ruth was walking to the door. "You'll finish that psalm and the drawing just as soon as we straighten this bedroom out in the morning. Do you hear me, Samuel?"

He closed his eyes. "Yes."

"Yes, what?"

"Yes, Ruth."

The trouble was, the longer Samuel thought on the problem, the further his thoughts traveled beyond the borders of reason. His ideas were wild and clever—at least he thought so—but they never could stand up to practical considerations. As such, the right answer always felt just out of reach.

"Turn off your lamp and go to sleep," Ruth said. "Good night to you."

Samuel did as he was told and the room surrendered to darkness.

For every question there is an answer, that's what his father used to tell him. Even if it's not the answer you were hoping for, it's still an answer, that's what he'd say. Samuel needed to find out what Ruth had done to his mother and for that he needed a way into her bedroom. So he could get hold of that diary. To show the world what a monster she was. A monster that would kill Robin Hood as easily as pulling a carrot from the garden and then trick Samuel into eating him. His mind was a whirlwind, pushing away the yawns and the weariness that crept up the bed toward him, trying all the while to hit on a solution. Something terrible had happened to his mother and the only way to prove it lay in Ruth's bedroom. He would not sleep until he had a solution. No matter what, he wouldn't sleep.

Samuel woke up with a start. "Mother?"

He blinked into the darkness. There had been laughter. He had heard his mother laughing. Had it been a dream? Yes, probably a dream, though in the fog of his mind he couldn't remember dreaming of her as he had before. It was as if that joyful cry had pushed itself under the door or through the keyhole and slipped into his ears. It was the laughter, its sweet heavenly music, which had drifted into his sleep and called him back.

Samuel closed his eyes again. It was just a dream, nothing more than—

The faint hum of voices breached the quiet and it made him sit up, reaching for the lamp, as if the light might help him to hear better. Light bloomed in the dark room and the clock said ten minutes past eleven. Samuel kept his hand on the lamp, not wishing to move a muscle or make any sound, not even the click of an elbow, as he strained to hear.

The voices dropped away and a peal of laughter, clear as church bells, lifted above it. His mother. Who else laughed with such abandon? It must be her. Samuel jumped from the bed.

The corridor churned with a sea of shadows, each one darker than the next, and Samuel had to run his hand along the wall to guide him through its dark tides. As he neared the landing, the murmur of voices seemed to thin out until there was only one, and by the time the boy crouched down and crept toward the banister, the gloomy hall perfectly matched to his spirits. His mother wasn't there at all, laughing her sweet laugh, delighted to be home. It was Ruth. Just Ruth. Standing there in her bathrobe, talking on the telephone in the rusted glow of an oil lamp.

"I'm not saying I won't come." Ruth had the telephone cord curled around her finger. "It's your wedding, Alice. I'm hardly going to miss that."

She was talking to her sister Alice, and that was a cruel blow.

"It's just that I haven't a thing to wear, and before you say it, I won't allow you to buy me a frock so don't even think of offering."

She laughed then, that beastly laugh that was so unlike her and sounded as if it had come from his mother.

"Wouldn't I look a fright in my work dress and apron? Don't worry, I'll think of something . . . Bring William? Don't be wicked, Alice. I've got more sense than to fall for that man's charms, such as they are." There was a pause. "Do I? Well, yes, I suppose I am a bit tired . . . The boy? Keeps me on my toes, same as always . . . I know, Alice, but what choice do I have? . . . I know, I know, it can't go on much longer. Yes, something has to be done."

Was he the boy she was speaking of? Samuel thought that he must be. Ruth chatted a little longer and then said her goodbyes, hanging up the phone. Then she picked up the oil lamp and began to climb the stairs. Samuel was already moving then. He crawled along the landing, then, when it was safe, ran down the corridor toward his bedroom. And as he went, he willed his bare feet to tread lightly on the boards so that Ruth would not hear him.

His bedroom door closed with hardly a sound of protest and Samuel tiptoed to the bed as quickly as he dared and arranged himself under the covers. He turned off the lamp and shut his eyes, listening. There wasn't a lot to hear. If not for the occasional crack of a floorboard, Samuel might have imagined Ruth was floating down the corridor. Or that she was standing very still and listening just as hard as he was. It didn't take long for the steady rhythm of her steps to make their mark on the stillness. Samuel heard her coming toward his door. He lay on his side and willed his eyes to not flicker when she came in to check on him.

But that didn't happen. What the boy heard was Ruth passing by without so much as a pause at his door. Then he heard the unmistakable sigh of a door opening somewhere down the corridor. And in the dead of night, with a head full of troubles, such a sigh couldn't go unheeded.

The boy moved quickly, his silhouette appearing and vanishing, as he passed the moonlit windows with their layers of milky dusk. At the very end of the hall, a soft glow framed the door. It was his mother's dressing room and, as it was the only light on in the entire hall, Ruth had to be there.

The floorboards seemed not to mind his light steps and made little noise. Ruth had been talking about him to her sister. *It can't go on much longer,* those were her words. *Something has to be done.* Samuel wasn't stupid, he knew what that meant.

Ruth wasn't going to keep him around. The time was up. She would do to him what she had done to his mother. What she had done to Robin Hood.

He reached the door and heard a faint sound, like a motor running low. Perhaps nobody in the whole world, except for Joseph, would believe the truth. They couldn't see what he could see, all the threads of lies and secrets that weaved around each other to make the whole blood-soaked tapestry. Ruth was a bad woman who had done horrible things. He knew that as surely as his name was Samuel Clay.

Ruth planned to murder him; she'd just confessed as much to her sister. Samuel had met Alice once and she had seemed nice enough, but now the boy understood that she had been putting on a show. She was just as wicked and nasty as Ruth. Probably they were in on it together.

Samuel dropped down on one knee and moved toward the keyhole. No one knew what Ruth was really like, not even his poor mother, who said Ruth was like her right arm. Now he was the only one left and he would have to stop her on his own.

If the boy was to guess what Ruth was doing in the dead of night in his mother's dressing room, he would have been wrong. For as he peered through the breach, his eyelashes brushing the brass plate of the doorknob, Samuel saw the flash of something red flicker to his left. Just a flash.

The oil lamp was set down on the couch where his mother liked to sit and put on her shoes and its faint glow captured only the middle part of the room. There was no sign of Ruth.

Samuel's eye fogged up and he blinked. And just like that she appeared, spinning into view. Yes, spinning. Ruth had his mother's red silk dress pressed over her bathrobe and she moved as if she were dancing, hugging the gown to herself. Samuel realized that the low sound he had heard was the housekeeper humming to herself.

She paused in front of the long mirror and looked at her reflection, just like his mother would, turning this way and that and stroking the fabric like it was a cat, humming all the while. Then Ruth closed her eyes and spun around, melting into the shadows.

31

"Hello?"

"Hello, Mrs. Collins."

"Who's this?" She sounded nervous. Or perhaps it was startled.

"It's Samuel, Mrs. Collins."

"Samuel? My goodness. Do you know what time it is?"

"Yes."

"What's got you calling at this hour?"

Samuel had the phone so close to his mouth the receiver was wet. "Could I speak to Joseph, please?"

"He's sleeping, love."

"Oh." Samuel swallowed, his eyes trained on the landing above for any sign of Ruth. "Could you wake him up, please? I know it's late but it's very important."

"I can't do that, Samuel."

Samuel took a shallow breath.

"As you say," continued Mrs. Collins, "it's awful late and you'd get no sense out of Joseph with a head full of sleep."

"I don't mind waiting for him to wake up."

"Is something wrong?"

"I just need to speak to Joseph."

"Maybe I can help? What's this about, Samuel?"

The boy said nothing.

"You should have been in bed hours ago," she said, "so I'm thinking there must be a very good reason you're calling Joseph at this time of night."

Wasn't that obvious? He had a reason. The most serious and bloody reason of all. But it was a reason that Mrs. Collins had found comical enough to laugh about with Ruth. Which is why he didn't answer her.

"What is it, Samuel?" she said.

"Nothing. It's only . . . I need to talk to Joseph."

"Is Ruth about? Let me have a word with her and I'm sure we can sort this out."

"No." Samuel said this firmly. "Ruth is asleep and nothing's wrong. I just wanted to have a talk with Joseph about school. We have to write out a psalm for the reverend and draw a picture and I wanted his help."

"Have you met my Joseph?" Mrs. Collins sounded amused. "He's hardly done a scrap of work on that thing himself. Anyway, I'm sure you can catch up with him tomorrow and work on it together." She laughed to herself. "Though I doubt you'll find him much help."

He needed to talk with his best friend. Now. Why couldn't she understand that? "Yes, that's a good idea."

"See, there's no need to sound so serious. I'll tell Joseph first thing in the morning."

Samuel's eyes swept back up to the landing where a heavy twilight had settled and he knew that anyone at all could be hiding within it. "Mrs. Collins, please don't tell Ruth I called."

"Well, all right."

Samuel heard the pockets of uncertainty in her voice. "Mrs. Collins, please don't tell Ruth. Please don't—it's very important."

"All right, Samuel." Her voice was softer now and wonderfully reassuring. "I won't tell her you called."

"Thank you, Mrs. Collins."

"Good night, Samuel."

The boy hung up the telephone.

32

It came to him just before sunrise. The solution he'd been waiting on. It had just wandered in among his swarming thoughts and sat down in the middle of the storm. He didn't pretend it would be easy—he wasn't stupid—but now that he had it in mind he knew he must act. All he had to do was wait until dawn.

The keyhole, that unblinking eye, hovered before the boy. Samuel closed one eye and moved closer. Ruth sat on the edge of the bed with her back to him, her hair spilling around her shoulders. Her head was bent forward just so and the boy wondered if perhaps she was praying. But then she gripped the back of her neck and rolled her head like she did whenever she had one of her headaches. She released a sigh, or perhaps it was a groan, and turned her head toward the side table. On it was the oil lamp, a picture of her father and a bottle that he thought might be wine.

Samuel's eyes shifted, glancing all the way down the hall. Everything was ready. He reached for the doorknob, but he wasn't careful about it and it shook with some force. He saw Ruth spin around and that's when he ran, tearing down the corridor. He heard Ruth's door open just as he reached the landing, twisting around the corner and pressing himself against the wall.

"Samuel?" From the sound of her voice, Ruth was probably scowling in his direction. "Samuel, I'm in no mood for games."

The sun was just waking, sifting through the trees outside and rendering the upper landing a patchwork of soft light and generous shade. The perfect place to steal a glimpse down the corridor. Samuel was sure she would see it at any moment.

With his hands pressed flat against the wall, the boy tilted his head, his right eye moving across the panels in a blur, then slipping free with a clear view down the corridor.

Ruth was turning already, looking the other way. And when she saw it, she took in a sharp breath and her hand went up to her mouth just as Samuel hoped it would. "Oh, Jesus," she whispered.

At the far end of the corridor was his mother's dressing room. The door was wide open, the whole chamber awash with morning light. She was standing in the middle of the room in the red silk dress, its rippling folds fixed tightly to her chest and the curves of her waist, the skirt spread out around her like a halo. The neck was slim and graceful but beyond it was nothing at all, matching the empty space at the end of her shoulders. The dust churned in the first blush of sunrise, its golden haze moving around her like the radiant glow of a headless ghost. The ghost of his mother.

The shock didn't have a grip on Ruth for long. It took just a moment or two for her to really see what had startled her so. It was just a mannequin, nothing more. But the fact that it wore the red silk dress, the very dress she had pressed to her own body the night before . . . well, that caused her to tuck the hair behind her ears and march down the corridor.

The boy watched, eyes rippling with curiosity and, yes, a little fear, as Ruth stormed toward the dressing room. "Samuel?" she barked.

He was running then, in her wake. She had reached the dressing room and Samuel could hear her stomping about inside. But he knew the room wouldn't hold her for long. Samuel willed his legs to quicken. He turned abruptly and darted through the open door. With a sharp right turn, he tucked himself behind the door and did his best not to make a sound. Ruth was once again in the corridor. He heard her move up the hall toward his bedroom, throwing the door open. She called his name several times but it didn't take her long to discover he wasn't in there, either.

"I hope you've had your fun, scaring me half to death." Her voice sounded scratched and rasping. "But I've had enough of your nonsense, Samuel Clay, and if you know what's good for you, you'll show yourself this instant!"

Through the seam of the door, he saw Ruth rushing past. Her eyes were wild and her mouth so tightly bunched it was barely a slit. The boy prayed to his mother that Ruth would keep walking—not stop and look inside the room where he was hiding.

"You're a wicked child, I know that much," she hissed.

Ruth had passed the door but then she stopped. Samuel saw the doorknob move. He heard her breathing, quick and short from the other side, and shut his eyes tight. Then the door closed with a bang. His whole body tensed, waiting for her to grab him. A key rattled in the lock. Samuel opened his eyes and found he was alone. Through the door, he heard Ruth walking away.

"I'll search every inch of this house if I have to," she hollered, her voice carrying up and down the corridor. "There's no running from me, Samuel, you should know that." A few more steps, then, "Show yourself!"

Her voice began to fade and Samuel supposed she was heading downstairs. The boy felt his shoulders relax and he took a deep breath, glancing around Ruth's bedroom. He figured that she had locked the door to stop him slipping inside while she was searching the house. The fact that it was locked was a problem—he couldn't pretend it wasn't—but there was always the window, though the drop was steep and he was sure he'd break his neck. Samuel didn't care. He had managed to find a way into Ruth's bedroom; he had done it all on his own, and the thrill of it tempered the cold fear stirring in his chest.

Ruth's secrets were locked in that very room. Now all he had to do was find them.

33

The desk under the window called to him. It was a small table, plain and unadorned, and Samuel reached it quickly, his attention fixed on the drawer. That's where Ruth had hidden the diary, the one in which she wrote down the terrible things she had done to his mother. The violence that had taken her from him.

He pulled on the drawer but his fingers caught. It was locked. Of course it was locked. Ruth was hardly going to keep a record of her dark deeds in an unlocked drawer. Samuel had no idea how long Ruth would keep looking for him, but as she was still in her nightgown, he knew she would return to her bedroom eventually. So he had to act quickly.

But how? Where would Ruth keep the key? Samuel's eyes swept around the small bedroom and a white apron stopped him dead. It was folded and hanging on the back of a chair by the wardrobe. The boy ran toward it, three thoughts whirling in his mind. First, Ruth kept all of the important house keys in the pocket of that apron. Two, wouldn't that have to include the one that opened the drawer where her gruesome crimes were recorded? Three, Ruth had just locked her bedroom door so did that mean all the keys were with her at that very moment?

Samuel scooped the apron up and, as he felt its weight, hope blossomed within him. His hand found the pocket, yanking it open. Down at the bottom was a pool of objects—a few hairpins, a set of keys on a single loop and something else. The silver clover pin that Ruth's father had given her. The one she said she had lost. More lies.

Samuel slipped the brooch into the pocket of his pajamas and hurried back to the desk with the keys. The one he needed was easy enough to find. The lock on the drawer was set into the wood, a thin slot, and only one key looked small enough to fit it. Samuel's hands quivered as he selected the key and pushed it into the chamber. He turned it and could hardly stop from gasping as the catch slipped away. Slowly, with greater care than was needed, Samuel pulled the drawer open. The boy looked down into this drawer and his mouth fell open, his eyes narrowed and dazed all at once. This is what he found. An ink pad and stamp. A pair of scissors. A container full of postage stamps, mostly American. A handful of postcards, each from cities in America and Canada. And something else—a folded piece of paper. What he didn't find was a diary.

A great mist blew up around Samuel's mind and it was as if he were watching everything from afar. He picked up a pile of the postcards—many were all blank. Others, like the one from Chicago and Florida, had been started and then abandoned, a crossed-out word here, an ink smudge there. All in his mother's delicate handwriting. The last postcard was from Boston and it was unfinished. Samuel turned it over several times, looking at it or through it, and it wasn't so much that he read the words, it was more that they lifted up and danced before him.

July 29, 1961
Dearest Samuel,
How slowly the days pass without you, my little man. I am still in Boston meeting with a great many boring bankers.
I long to have this business over with so that I can get home to you but I fear

It ended there in midsentence. Ruth hadn't finished writing it yet. The ground seemed to shift under Samuel, moving or dropping away, and he reached out and grabbed the desk. Ruth had written the postcards. She had killed his mother, truly killed her—all this time, the postcards and the promises, these were all the threads of her duplicity. The whole thing, it was all her.

The boy's hands churned through the drawer, turning every postcard over. What he was looking for he didn't know. A folded page at the bottom buckled and flipped onto the ground and Samuel scooped it up. The page was handwritten and numbered in the top right-hand corner. *Four.* Page number four. He hurried at the words.

> him but it doesn't come easily, and the harder I try, the less I feel.
>
> Does that make me sound a monster? Dr. Boyle says it will come in time and that I must be patient. My darling, I hope you will be patient, too. Samuel is very lucky to have such a wonderful father and I hope that once I am rested, the sun will shine on our little family and I will find my place in it.
>
> With love and kisses,
Margot

At the bottom of the page some of the words had been written out several times—*love and kisses, Samuel, my*—trying, it seemed, to get the shape and angle of the handwriting just so. He read the first line again.

> him but it doesn't come easily, and the harder I try, the less I feel.

Samuel thought back to the letter hidden in the atlas. The letter with the missing page. The missing page four. In his mind's eye, the last sentence of page three scratched across the darkness.

I do so want to love . . .

Then it fixed itself, like a link in the chain, to the first line of the page in his hand.

I do so want to love him but it doesn't come easily, and the harder I try, the less I feel.

She was writing about him. Wanting to love him but not being able to. His head was shaking, moving from side to side the way you do when something is utterly false. As he stared at the letter, the words began to curl around each other like a nest of serpents. Like a swarm of lies.

Perhaps Samuel did hear the key rattle in the door behind him and the faint screech as it swung open. But if he did, it wasn't enough to bring him back.

"So, now you know." That's what she said. She didn't sound angry or even upset. "I suppose it was only a matter of time."

Samuel didn't turn around. "It was all you."

"The postcards?" Samuel heard Ruth walking toward him. "Yes, I wrote them."

"It was all you," Samuel said again.

She struck swiftly and from behind, slapping Samuel across the side of his head. The boy stumbled, and before he could find his feet,

Ruth had him pinned against the wardrobe, her hand pushing hard against his chest. "What right have you to go through my things? Have you no shame?" Spit flew from her mouth, hitting Samuel in the eye. "After all I've done for you, how dare you violate my quarters like a common thief."

Samuel pushed on her but it was as if she were made of stone.

"You killed my mother!" he shouted. "You killed her and then you wrote those cards so I would think she was in America. I was right . . ." He tried not to cry but the grief rose up and claimed him. "I didn't want to be right but I was and now I know what you've done. I know—"

"What do you know? That I've looked after you the best way I know how, while your mother was nowhere to be found? Even when she was here, she wasn't."

"Shut up!"

"That's what's true, Samuel. Yes, I've been writing those cards, someone had to. Your own mother could surely never be bothered. When I saw how much they meant to you, how your eyes lit up when you got one, well, I kept on writing them. You missed her so fiercely. Those cards were about the only thing that seemed to make it bearable. For you and for me."

Samuel brought his knee up as hard as he could. Ruth groaned and her grip slackened, which was chance enough for Samuel to ram her with his shoulder, knocking her sideways. He ran to the desk and picked up the letter.

"You are a poisonous monster," he shouted. "That's why you wrote that stupid letter—you wanted me to think that Mother didn't love me, that she was a beast like you. Like you, Ruth! Who hates the ones she's supposed to love and wants them to take a gun down to the henhouse and kill themselves."

Ruth used the wall to get to her feet. "Your mind is a malignant thing, Samuel, and it's eaten what little sense you had. I used that letter to learn her handwriting and nothing more."

"Liar!"

"Do you want honesty, Samuel?" She wiped her mouth and moved toward him. "Your mother never took to you. You wanted so much of her, following her around, clinging to her like a monkey on a vine, and it suffocated her. Neither of you could win, you see? The more she tried to keep you at arm's length, the more desperately you wanted to be near her."

"You murdered her to keep her away from me," Samuel whispered.

"She didn't know how to be a mother. Not every woman does." Ruth shrugged. "Mine didn't. It's not their fault and it's not ours, either, it's just what is."

Samuel swallowed but his throat was bone-dry.

"I saw you with Mother's dress, dancing around like a lunatic. You killed her and now you're trying to take her place."

For the briefest moment something bright flashed across Ruth's face. She half smiled. "Your mother knew I had my sister's wedding in the autumn and she told me I was welcome to that dress. She said the color was garish and she'd never wear it again."

Samuel saw the lies easily enough; they practically leached from her skin like poisonous gas. She twisted everything, turning the truth in on itself until it looked like something else. And she would have to be punished—not just hung, which she surely would be, but something that might hurt even more. That's why he pulled the clover pin from his pocket.

Ruth lifted her hand when she saw it. "Give that to me."

She made a move to grab it and Samuel stepped back, holding it between his fingers. "Olive said it wasn't real and I can feel that it would snap easily enough in my hands."

"Don't." The panic was alive in her dark eyes. "My father gave me that and—"

"You wanted him dead," said Samuel. "That's what you said, wasn't it? You were happy he died because you have a black heart. You killed Robin Hood. You kill everything."

"I didn't kill your mother, Samuel." Ruth took

a step toward him. "I would never hurt her."

The boy felt the fear slipping away from him, replaced by an utter stillness. "You hurt me easily enough. Beat me."

He pressed his fingers together and the cheap pin began to bend.

"Please!" She had her hands out in front of her like she was trying to feel her way in the dark. "I know I haven't always treated you as I should have. I don't have that way about me with children, I never have. When I left home, I didn't become a governess or a schoolteacher. I became a housekeeper so that I would be at arm's length from all of that. But then I came here and I found myself in a house run on credit and bad promises. Your mother needed me to keep you busy and I did. Before I knew it, I was doing just about everything for you. I didn't seek the duty but it was there and who else was going to do it if I didn't? Your father? He spent most of his time in Lincolnshire trying to hold things together. There was little money to pay my wages, let alone a nanny to take proper care of you."

It was all so wrong, so awful and untrue and wicked. *I do so want to love him but it doesn't come easily.* They were Ruth's horrid words. His mother did love him, she did want to be with him, she hadn't left him in the dead of night and gone abroad. It was all Ruth, every bit of it.

So he said, "Murderer."

The pin snapped easily enough, bending quickly, the thin metal buckling, then splitting down the middle.

She flew at him, her face a mask of such fury it hardly looked like her. Samuel took off, running for the door. But Ruth was too quick. She grabbed the back of his head, catching his hair. She pulled with such force he reeled back, slamming into the side table, his ribs flushed with pain, the skin splitting on his arm.

"You're right!" Ruth turned and nodded her head, panting loudly. "I killed her. What use was she to you? Margot Clay wasn't a real mother, not like I was."

Samuel was still on the ground and something about hearing the truth, the heartbreaking truth, numbed the pain and fixed him to the spot.

"Didn't I do all the taking care of, all the cleaning up after, all the tending to?" Ruth sniffed, her top lip curling. "I did everything while your mother did her best to pretend you didn't exist. Then she tells me I'm to be let go. Can you imagine? After all my years of faithful service? So I let *her* go." Ruth waved her hand in the air. "All gone."

The boy began to cry. "No."

"Oh, yes. Poisoned her tea, I did. Then I had William help me drag her down to the river by Braddon Hall. Stuffed her in a laundry bag, loaded her up with stones and pushed her in."

Ruth smirked. "She was made of stone and she sank like one."

"I hate you!"

He got to his feet and charged toward her, his arms flailing about. Ruth tried to push him away but he was a wild thing, kicking and punching. When Ruth grabbed his neck, he sunk his teeth into her arm. She cried out and brought her fist down on his face. Samuel stumbled, tripping over the bed, and Ruth swooped down and pulled him up by the hair and he saw in that moment that she planned to kill him just as she had his mother.

Ruth's hand found his throat again and Samuel struck quickly, grabbing the wine bottle and swinging it at her head. The bottle didn't break but Ruth cried out and that's when Samuel charged at her, pushing her back. He ran past the desk, bound for the door, but her hand snared the back of his pajama top.

"You devil," she spat.

She meant to finish him. He knew that. It wasn't planned, what he did next. Samuel felt her reeling him in and he glimpsed the scissors in the open drawer—just lying there. He reached for them just as Ruth was yanking him back. She spun him around and, as she did, he lifted the blades. Just like that, they found a place in her chest. Ruth took one sharp breath, like someone had just splashed cold water on her face.

Samuel pulled the scissors out and blood

seeped across the gray nightgown like a stain. Ruth's eyes were wide and pierced but no sound came out. The boy looked down at the scissors, then up at Ruth, not sure if he could believe what he was seeing. Ruth's legs gave out and she dropped all at once to the floor, her hand pressed to the bleeding wound on her chest.

"Samuel." Her voice had lost its violence. "Please, Samuel . . . help me."

The boy stepped back. "You killed Mother."

She was shaking her head and a cry came up and out of her. "I was angry at you . . . that's all. I didn't harm your mother . . ." She gulped, her eyes shutting with the pain. "I was angry and I said the one thing I knew would hurt you the most."

Now it was Samuel who was shaking his head. "Mother loves me. You took her away."

"I didn't, child." Blood oozed around her fingers. "I didn't kill her. Help me, please."

"I won't."

With a great shudder, Ruth used her free arm to push herself up. She got to her knees, her pale face a knot of pain. "Your mother is alive, Samuel. She's alive."

"Lies," said the boy.

Using the bed, Ruth found a way to her feet, but her head seemed to whirl and she stumbled, falling over the desk. Samuel ran from the room then, still holding the scissors. He feared that

Ruth would grab them and murder him just as she had his mother and he also feared that if he stayed she would spin her story and twist his thoughts. Ruth had murdered his mother. She wrote the postcards and that beastly letter.

If you only knew how wretched I feel when he is clinging to me and calling for me over and over.

They were Ruth's words. She wanted him to believe that his mother hated having him close. That his love for her was a great burden she hadn't the strength to carry.

I feel as if I cannot breathe.

His mother loved him best of all.

I feel as if I am being pulled under the waves.

It was all a pack of lies.

You wanted so much of her, following her around, clinging to her like a monkey on a vine, and it suffocated her.

It was all Ruth, the whole wicked thing.

As Samuel ran, he heard Ruth call out from behind him. He guessed she had made it out into the corridor. He didn't look back but he understood she was coming after him. Hunting him. Not ever stopping. Because that's what killers do.

"Samuel, come back!"

Her soul was black. Black as night. So black that she was glad that her father had killed himself and so black that she had killed Samuel's mother. Taken her away from him and then tried to make him believe that it was his mother who wanted to be far from him. That she went all the way to America and hadn't written to him once. That she couldn't bear to be near him.

I do so want to love him but it doesn't come easily.

There wasn't a mother in the world that didn't want to be near her child. He knew that. Mothers love you and take care of you and fret awfully when you were far from them or even in the next room. Mothers love their children; they don't have a choice about it.

I feel as if I cannot breathe . . .

Ruth thought he would be stupid enough to think his mother never took to him. That she was always unthreading his hands from around her waist, always pushing him away, always running from him.

I feel as if I am being pulled under the waves.

Death was the thing keeping her from Samuel. Death was the only thing that could have.

"Samuel." Ruth was gasping. "Samuel, stop!"

The boy looked back. Ruth was halfway down the corridor, the front of her nightdress soaked in blood, her body slumped against the wall. And he saw in her agony, the blood and the feebleness, that it was Ruth's violence that had felled her. He had done what he had to do to stop her. His mother deserved nothing less.

The boy ran across the landing and took to

271

the stairs. He didn't know where he was going, he just knew that he was getting away from the butcher who had taken everything good from him. Who had tried to turn his mother into something she wasn't. A mother who didn't want him to visit her in Bath. A mother who wished to be anywhere but with him. A mother who would sail to America for one hundred and twenty-one days and never once care enough to write. Such a woman could never be his mother. She would be a monster.

As Samuel charged down the stairs, he saw that the front door was open. He saw the bags upon the floor and the fluttering of her yellow dress, like the wings of a bird, and heard the unmistakable music of her voice.

"It's such a glorious morning, I decided to walk from the station."

The sunlight spilled in and pushed all around her and she glowed and shimmered as if she and the sunrise were one and the same. Like a ghost or something.

I do so want to love him but it doesn't come easily.

The boy didn't know if she was real or make-believe. He only knew that if she were there, really there, then she must have been away. Away for all that time and in her absence, her silence, this great emptiness had grown up inside of him.

I do so want to love him . . .

And this emptiness had made his thoughts sickly and his heart ache.

I do so want to love him but it doesn't come easily.

He heard Ruth calling his name from the top of the stairs. She had been right about everything? The lies weren't lies at all. His mother looked at him and then at Ruth, the smile slipping from her face. He could feel the scissors in his hand, his fingers curled tightly around them. The boy's mind, a malignant thing, grew quiet and still then. Perhaps he didn't understand what it all meant. He only knew he was running at her and that it was too late to stop.

34

The room was bare, just a table and a few chairs. Two cups sat on the table, both tea, one white and one black. Ruth was on one side and Detective Rowe on the other. She had a handbag perched on her lap and was wearing a gray dress and a small black hat.

"Thank you for taking the time to come down, Miss Tupper," said the detective.

"I don't recall being given a choice."

"It's what happens in an investigation. I'm sure you understand we still have questions."

"I don't doubt that, Detective, but this is the third time I've been interrogated, and I can assure you, my answers will be the same as they were the last time and the time before that."

The boy sat on a chair outside. He had his favorite red fighter plane in his hand and if you looked at him you might think he was admiring it. But he wasn't. The door was closed—it always was—but as the room was little more than an empty box, the voices carried right to him.

Detective Rowe lit another cigarette and took a long drag. He was neatly dressed in a dark suit and his face was almost handsome, but his teeth were starting to yellow, which did him no favors. "Let's go back to Sunday, September the twenty-fourth. What can you tell me about that morning?"

"It was like any other as I've said over and again. I got up, got dressed and then saw to breakfast."

"And the boy?"

"Samuel woke at the usual time, right with the sun. We spoke upstairs, briefly. I reminded him to finish his homework and to clean up his bedroom and then I went downstairs to the kitchen. Samuel came down not long after and we ate breakfast together."

"No one came to the door?"

"Not a soul."

"Did you venture outside at all?"

"Not until lunchtime." Ruth was wearing gloves and her fingers were locked together. "I had to go into the village and make a delivery to Mrs. Pryce, the reverend's wife."

The detective looked down at the notes in front of him. "Mrs. Pryce said you had hurt your shoulder."

"Yes." Ruth straightened her back. "I slipped in the bath the night before, nothing serious."

"Mrs. Pryce said you seemed to be in a lot of pain."

"Not really. As I've told you before, it was just a cut and luckily Samuel helped me bandage it and the wound healed quickly. Though why my injured shoulder would be of any interest to you, I can't imagine."

The detective looked at Ruth for a long moment. Then he said, "Samuel didn't go with you?"

"Where?"

"To make the delivery to Mrs. Pryce."

"No, I told him to stay at the house and finish his schoolwork—he had a psalm to write. I was gone less than an hour."

"While you were out, you didn't see any sign of Mrs. Clay?"

"No, I did not. Detective Rowe, with great respect, what is it you think I'm keeping from you?"

The detective stubbed out his cigarette. "We know that Mrs. Clay boarded the overnight train from London on Saturday, September the twenty-third, and we know she got off at Penzance around six on Sunday morning and then boarded another train to the village. She told a porter to send her trunks up to the house and she left the station with two small bags and an umbrella."

"Yes, I know the story, Detective."

"That was three and a half months ago, Miss Tupper, and there's been no sign of Mrs. Clay since. The last sighting we have of her is a witness who saw her entering the woods across from the station."

"Then look for her there."

"We have." Detective Rowe picked at his front tooth. "Your mistress seems to have vanished into

a puff of smoke. But people don't just disappear, Miss Tupper."

"Yes, I realize that, Detective Rowe, but if you think I'm hiding her away, then you are sorely mistaken." She was scowling. "Though you should know that better than anyone. You've searched the house high and low."

"All right, then, Miss Tupper, what do you think happened to her?"

Ruth cleared her throat. "I wouldn't know about that. What I do know is that Mrs. Clay had a world of trouble and a gift for running away from it."

"Seems to me she was in America to try and fix her troubles."

"From what you tell me, Mrs. Clay's trip wasn't a great success. Isn't it a fact that she couldn't raise the money she was after?"

"What's your point, Miss Tupper?"

"Only this—the house is mortgaged to the eyeballs and up for sale, the company is in default and, as far as I can tell, Mrs. Clay was about as broke as a person can be. I don't know that I would blame her if she has run off."

"What about the boy?" The detective sat back in his chair and folded his arms. "What kind of mother would run off and leave her son?"

Ruth sighed. "Mrs. Clay never took to Samuel as I've told you time and again. She even went to doctors about it and you can check that if you like. All those months in America and she never once wrote to him. You tell me, Detective Rowe, what kind of a mother is that?"

"Ah, yes, the postcards." His smile was boyish. "You wrote to Samuel pretending to be his mother. Bit strange, wouldn't you say?"

"Strange? I'd call it merciful. All Samuel did was pine for her and I couldn't bear to see him so upset." She touched her hat, pushing it slightly to the left. "So I did what I could to ease his suffering."

"You lied to him."

"And I would do it again. I found the book of postcards in a secondhand shop in Penzance a few weeks after Mrs. Clay left for America. Samuel was already asking after her a hundred times a day and coming across those cards felt like a gift from God above." She allowed a faint smile. "Learning to copy her handwriting was a challenge but I'm a quick study."

"I bet you are."

Ruth huffed. "After that, it was just a matter of stamping the postmark, just the date all smudged over, and slipping one in with the mail every few weeks. Mrs. Clay had mentioned a few of the places she intended to visit so I thought it best to keep her moving about, going here and there." Ruth met the detective's gaze. "There's no crime in trying to make a child feel better, is there, Detective?"

Detective Rowe peered down at his notes. "We spoke to a Mrs. Collins. She said that Samuel told her son . . ." He scanned the page. "Joseph. Samuel told Joseph that he thought you had killed his mother and . . . where is it? . . . oh, yes, hid her body in the cellar." The detective looked up at Ruth. "Where would he get such an idea, Miss Tupper?"

"Where do boys get most of their ideas, Detective? Samuel has a wild imagination and I think you'll find that it was that fool of a boy, Joseph Collins, who planted that particular bit of nonsense in Samuel's head."

"Maybe so. What I can't work out is why Samuel would be so willing to believe you could hurt his mother."

Ruth sniffed, shifting in her seat. "A child's mind is full of conspiracies. As I just said, Mrs. Clay had been gone for months—poor Samuel counted the days—and I think it was somehow easier for him to think somebody had . . . done something to his mother than to imagine the truth. That she had gone away and left him."

"But she hadn't left him, had she? Mrs. Clay caught the train back and had her trunks sent up to the house. She was coming home, Miss Tupper."

"Well, she never made it, Detective. That is what I've been telling you for months."

There was a knock at the door.

"Yes?" snapped Detective Rowe.

A constable stepped in. "Got that witness from the Barker Street robbery out front."

"Tell him to wait."

"Thing is, sir, Mr. Norris says he's got to catch a train at two o'clock—something about his sick daughter."

"Tell him to wait."

"Yes, sir."

The constable was closing the door when Detective Rowe called him back. "Send the boy in." He shifted his gaze to Ruth. "No objections, I take it?"

"I object very much." Ruth sat forward. "He is a nine-year-old boy whose mother has vanished. I think he's been through more than enough, don't you?"

"It's just a few questions, Miss Tupper."

There was a murmur of voices and then Samuel walked into the room and took the seat next to Ruth. The boy and the housekeeper did not look at each other.

"Hello, Samuel," said Detective Rowe. "Remember me?"

Samuel nodded.

"I'm trying to find out what's happened to your mother," said the detective. "You want me to do that, don't you, Samuel?"

The boy nodded.

"Do you remember the day when Miss Tupper

went into the village to make a delivery to Mrs. Pryce?"

"Yes."

"Was there something different about that day, Samuel? Something out of the ordinary?"

"Ruth had hurt her shoulder and I had to pack the lemon tarts and the tea cakes in boxes for her."

"You saw Ruth fall, did you?"

"No. She was in the bath. But I heard her cry out."

"When was this?"

"The night before."

"What time?"

Samuel shrugged. "I was in bed."

The detective looked down at the file. "So, back to the day Ruth made the delivery to Mrs. Pryce—she left you home by yourself, did she?"

Samuel nodded.

"And while you were there all by yourself, did anyone come to the house?"

"Just Mr. Watson from the station." The boy placed the red fighter plane on the edge of the desk. "He brought Mother's trunks."

"Nobody else?" said the detective.

Samuel shook his head.

"You never saw your mother?" Detective Rowe rubbed his left ear until it was red. "Maybe you saw someone that looked like her? Or maybe a stranger? Someone you'd never seen before?"

"I didn't see anyone."

"Nobody knocked on the door besides Mr. Watson?"

Samuel shook his head again.

"You didn't see anything unusual outside? Didn't hear any strange noises? A car, maybe? Or someone crying out?"

"No." Samuel pushed the hair from his eyes. "I was doing my homework."

"The day I'm asking you about, Samuel, the day the trunks were delivered—your mother had caught an overnight train from London. Did you know that?"

Samuel nodded.

Detective Rowe said, "She was coming home."

"Yes."

"What happened to her, do you think?"

"How can the boy answer such a question, Detective?" Ruth's voice had all the sharp edges. "If you haven't any decency, at least show some sense."

"I'm just asking Samuel what he thinks, that's all." The detective lit another cigarette and Samuel watched it seethe into life. "Where do you suppose your mother is right now, Samuel?"

The boy watched the smoke coil up from the cigarette, and it made him think of Ruth cutting the baked potato and blowing on the steam.

"Samuel?" said Detective Rowe.

"I think she is resting," said Samuel.

"That's enough." Ruth hit the table, which made Samuel jump. "I won't allow this cruelty to continue. What would a boy of his age know about such things? Shame on you, Detective Rowe."

Another knock at the door.

Detective Rowe flicked the embers from his cigarette into an ashtray. "Yes?"

The same constable, looking sheepish, stuck his head around the door. "Sorry, sir. Mr. Norris says he can't wait any longer and if you can't talk to him now, well, he'll—"

"Bloody hell." The detective closed the folder. "Tell him I'll be right there." He regarded Ruth coolly. "I suppose we're done, but I daresay I'll be wanting to talk to you again."

"Detective Rowe, you may be done with me but I am not done with you."

"I'd love to sit here and chat but, as you heard, I have a witness to interview."

The detective stood up and so did Ruth.

"I have a few things to say," she said, threading her handbag along her wrist, "and as the person in charge of Samuel's welfare for the present moment, I have every right to speak on his behalf. He should not be subject to any more of this—"

"I thought there was other family?" The detective was collecting his file and didn't sound especially interested. "An uncle or something?"

"Yes." Ruth's voice dropped to a whisper,

which seemed silly. "Samuel does have an uncle but he . . . he's unwilling to take the boy on full-time. There's also a grandfather in America."

"He's going to live over here, is he? Poor sod."

Ruth glanced down at the boy. "Samuel will stay here in England and continue his schooling, though where that will be I'm not sure." She cleared her throat. "As for the holidays, America is very far to travel, and Samuel's grandfather thinks it best that he stays here."

Detective Rowe took a long drag of his cigarette. "You're looking after him, are you?"

"Well." Ruth moved the straps of her handbag and seemed to have trouble finding a position that satisfied her. "That's still to be worked out."

Samuel turned the plane over in his hands.

"Like that, is it?" said the detective with a smirk.

"I beg your pardon?"

The constable reappeared at the door. "Sorry again, sir, but Mr. Norris says—"

"Impatient bugger." The detective stubbed out the cigarette. "I'm on my way."

When Detective Rowe headed for the door, Ruth followed after him.

"I have more to say, Detective, things that Samuel need not be troubled by. May I walk with you?"

There were things to discuss. And Samuel was just a boy.

The detective sighed. "If you must."

He walked quickly and Ruth hurried in his tracks. But she stopped in the doorway. Samuel heard her clear her throat the way she always did. The boy felt her looking at him but he didn't turn around. He guessed what he might see if he did and he knew what it would mean. Turning around was an act of bravery and he had no courage left.

"Stay here, Samuel," Ruth said. "I'll come back for you."

She closed the door and it hardly made a sound. He waited to hear her go but all was silent. Then he became aware of the ticking clock, its crisp drumbeat, and the sound of his breaths, faint and slow. He wanted to get up and go to her. To see that stern look in her eyes and hear the certainty in her voice and know that it wasn't the end. That she wouldn't leave. But then he heard her heels on the floor outside and Samuel understood the moment had passed. Ruth's footsteps were rapid as she walked down the hall to catch Detective Rowe, fading a little with every step. She was headed someplace else now, moving away from him.

ACKNOWLEDGMENTS

The impulse to write this book came suddenly but not without warning. I first had the idea over twenty years ago as a budding scriptwriter, and despite it going nowhere, the story of a boy and a housekeeper lingered patiently in my imagination, waiting for me to try again. When I did, the words seemed to fly out in a hurry, as if they feared I might change my mind.

For such a solitary pursuit, a great many people are involved in the life of a writer. My agent, Madeleine Milburn, has taken my stories out into the world and has been a tireless champion of my literary whims. Also at the MM office are a fantastic team including Giles Milburn, Haley Steed and Alice Sutherland-Hawes.

I worked with two editors on this book who were determined to bring out the best in my writing. John Glynn at Hanover Square Press led me through the process with insight and ease. Thanks also to executive VP Loriana Sacilotto, VP Margaret Marbury-O'Neill, editorial director Peter Joseph, senior marketing manager Randy Chan, senior marketing director Amy Jones and publicist Emer Flounders.

Kimberley Atkins at Penguin Random House Australia has sharp instincts and I thank her for brilliantly suggesting the ill-fated rabbit. Thanks also to Kathryn Knight and Alex Ross.

My parents have been a huge support as I navigate this crazy business and I owe them a great debt. Thanks also to Christine, Carol and Paul for support and encouragement. And lastly, thank you to Jacqui, dear friend since '93.

Center Point Large Print
600 Brooks Road / PO Box 1
Thorndike, ME 04986-0001 USA

(207) 568-3717

US & Canada:
1 800 929-9108
www.centerpointlargeprint.com